THE SEVEN CLUES

Norris Jordan uncovers a fiendish plot and is about to give evidence to the British Government — but on his return to England he is murdered. Having anticipated this, however, he has concealed his evidence within an elaborate series of riddles, each leading to a scrap of vital information; the first going to his friend, Peter Clayton. Aided by the head of the Secret Service, Clayton struggles to solve the riddles — but the duo soon find that their very lives are at stake as the plotters try to silence them . . .

GERALD VERNER

♦

THE SEVEN CLUES

Complete and Unabridged

LINFORD
Leicester

First published in Great Britain

First Linford Edition
published 2014

A catalogue record for this book is available
from the British Library.

ISBN 978–1–4448–2015–7

Published by
F. A. Thorpe (Publishing)
Anstey, Leicestershire

Set by Words & Graphics Ltd.
Anstey, Leicestershire
Printed and bound in Great Britain by
T. J. International Ltd., Padstow, Cornwall

This book is printed on acid-free paper

1

The Man with the Secret

Peter Clayton yawned, laid aside his book and, hoisting himself out of the chair, stretched himself wearily. The hands of the small clock on the mantelpiece pointed to a quarter to twelve, which meant that the time was really a quarter past eleven since no amount of adjustment on Peter's part had ever succeeded in keeping the clock right for more than six hours at a stretch.

Walking over to the window, he pulled aside the curtains and stared out into the dripping darkness of the little cottage garden. It was still raining heavily, the hiss and splash of it on the leaves and bushes came to his ears, and after a moment or two he turned disgustedly away, letting the curtains fall and blot out the depressing vision. This was the third day of almost continuous rain, and since fine weather is at least to be expected in the middle of June, Peter's annoyance was not unreasonable.

Going back to the table in the centre of the cosy sitting room, he poured himself out a whisky and soda, drank half of it, and stood with the remainder of it in his hand, debating whether he should continue his not very interesting book, or go to bed in the hope that the morrow would produce a change.

Five years previously he had been a reporter attached to the staff of one of the London dailies, and he would have been the first to admit that he had not been a very good reporter. His inclination lay more in the direction of fiction than fact, and when an aunt had died, leaving him a respectable legacy, he had given up his job without a pang of regret.

The cottage nestling among the Berkshire Hills had been almost his first purchase. He was a lover of the country, and it had always been his ambition to settle down in some quiet spot where he could occupy his time with a little gardening and a little golf, and write when the mood took him. It must be admitted that the mood seldom did take him, for although he loved to indulge in long and leisurely walks through the leafy lanes and woods that surrounded his small domain, and occupy his mind with working out sensational plots, he seldom summoned up sufficient energy to put the results of his imagination on paper. In the small bureau which occupied a corner of the sitting room were a score or so of half finished novels, novels which he had begun in a sudden excess of energy and tired of before they were half completed. It was lucky for him that his small income provided the necessities of life without the need of working, for this desultory method of authorship would have brought him little or no return.

He stood for some minutes twisting the glass in his fingers. He was not so much tired as thoroughly bored, and the only outlet for his boredom seemed to lie in the direction of bed. He came to a decision, finished his drink, set the tumbler down on the table and set about locking up for the night.

He lived entirely alone, his few wants being attended to by a woman who came in every day from the neighbouring village and did such cleaning as was necessary.

Going into the small and spotless kitchen he bolted the back door, latched the window, and was coming back along the low-roofed passage which led to the front entrance when he heard a sound which brought him to a sudden stop. Above the monotonous hiss of the rain came the unmistakable crunch of feet on the wet gravel. Somebody was coming up the little path from the gate, which gave admittance to the roadway.

Peter frowned and listened in wonder. Who could it be at this hour of the night? The cottage was an isolated one; the roadway passing its small gate was narrow and unused. Few people came that way, even in daylight.

The footsteps grew more distinct, hurried, uneven footsteps, as though the person who made them was half running. Right up to the porch they came, and the little knocker was wielded by an impatient hand.

Peter hesitated for the fraction of a second, and then, going quickly forward, opened the door. As he peered out expectantly, the dim figure of a man loomed out of the darkness and pushed past him into the narrow passage.

'Here, what the dickens — ' began Peter indignantly, but the newcomer interrupted him.

'Shut the door, Clayton!' he panted, in a hoarse, breathless whisper. 'Shut the door!'

Peter obeyed mechanically. He had no idea who this midnight intruder was — it was dark in the passage, and he could see little of his visitor beyond a soft hat and a dripping mackintosh — but he apparently knew Peter's name

'Bolt the door and put up the chain — if you've got one!' said the man urgently, and then, as Peter began to protest: 'Don't argue, old chap, do as I ask; I'll explain later!'

Completely bewildered, but conscious of an intense curiosity, Peter bolted and chained the door.

'Now,' he said, as he led the way to the lighted sitting room, 'perhaps you'll tell me who you are and what is the meaning of this little joke?'

'It's anything but a joke, I assure you, Clayton,' replied the visitor gravely as he removed his wet hat and rain-soaked mackintosh and flung them on a chair.

'Good Lord!' breathed Peter in amazement as he saw the other's face fully for the first time. 'It's Norris Jordan!'

The late caller nodded.

'I wondered how long it'd be before you recognized me,' he said. 'Can I have a drink?'

Peter pointed silently to the table, too astonished to speak. Picking up the decanter, Jordan poured himself out half a glass of neat whisky with a hand that shook slightly.

'That's better,' he sighed, when he had swallowed it, and a tinge of colour crept into his pale, gaunt cheeks. Pulling a pipe and pouch from his pocket he flung himself into a chair and began to stuff tobacco into the bowl with nervous fingers. 'Surprised to see me, eh?' he said. 'I expect you are. I only landed in England this morning.'

Surprised was a mild description of Peter's feelings. It was at least ten years since he had seen Norris Jordan. Jordan had been political correspondent attached to a rival paper for a short period, and it was during this time that Peter had met him. A fine linguist, possessing a comfortable income of his own, he had travelled round Europe picking up stray items of information which formed the basis for the articles which occasionally appeared under his name.

Watching the gaunt figure of the man sprawling in his easy chair, puffing irregularly at the pipe he had lighted, Peter recalled the circumstances surrounding his extraordinary disappearance and silence.

One morning in late autumn, ten years before, he had shut up his London flat and vanished, none knew whither. Since that time no one had heard anything of him, no articles had been received, no communications to show where he was or what he was doing. The general theory among his Fleet Street acquaintances was that he had poked his nose into business that did not concern him once too often, and had suffered for his curiosity.

Now, on this wet June night, he had reappeared as suddenly as he had vanished, in this little cottage among the Berkshire Hills. It was not surprising that Peter was astonished, and put that astonishment into words.

'Where the dickens did you spring from?' he demanded when he had recovered his voice.

Jordan looked at him through a cloud of smoke, the old quizzical smile curving his thin lips.

'Spring is hardly the right word,' he began. 'I — '

He stopped abruptly, sitting up with a jerk, his expression one of alert watchfulness.

'What was that?' he whispered quickly.

'What was what?' said Peter. 'There's nothing — '

Jordan held up his hand to stop him.

'Quiet!' he muttered under his breath. 'Listen!'

Peter listened, but he could hear nothing except the steady patter of the rain. 'What did you think you heard?' he asked.

Jordan did not reply at once. Getting up quickly he moved softly over to the table and put out the lamp, plunging the room into darkness.

'I could have sworn I heard a stealthy footstep,' he muttered, and Peter saw that his lean face was bedewed with perspiration. 'I must have been mistaken.'

'Of course you were mistaken,' said Peter. 'Who the deuce do you think is likely to be wandering about my garden at this hour of the night and in the rain — '

Jordan picked up his pipe and looked at it queerly.

'You think I'm crazy,' he said. 'I suppose it looks that way to you, but I was never saner in my life.'

Peter eyed him doubtfully. The thought had crossed his mind but there was nothing in Jordan's appearance to justify it. His face was haggard and he looked like a man who was on the verge of a breakdown, but there was nothing of madness in the steady eyes that returned Peter's gaze.

'I suppose,' he went on, 'that since I've butted in on you at this ungodly hour and behaved like the leading character in a shilling shocker, I ought to offer some explanation.' He knocked the half consumed tobacco out of his pipe and began to refill it jerkily. 'I can't tell you the whole story, it would take too long, but there are certain people, Clayton, who would sleep more peacefully if they knew I was dead!' He struck a match and held it to the bowl of his pipe, sucking in the smoke as though it had a soothing effect on his nerves. 'I've no doubt,' he continued, 'that in company with several of my friends you wondered why I disappeared so suddenly ten years ago. Well, I'll tell you, and then you'll realize that my fears are not as imaginary as they seem. You know how fond I was of digging down into the political undercurrents of Europe?'

Peter nodded.

'Well, I dug down further than I expected,' said Jordan. He spoke rapidly and unevenly, his eyes straying every now and again to the curtained window. 'Quite by accident I stumbled on the beginning of a plot which, even now, I can scarcely realize is not the figment of a nightmare.

'I got first hint of it in an obscure little café in Budapest and my insatiable curiosity made me follow it up. The clues led me half over the world, from Budapest to Vienna, from Vienna to Berlin, from Berlin to Russia, and from there to a small state in the Balkans and a score of other queer and out-of-the-way places. It took me nine and a half years to acquire my information, and during that time I carried my life in my hands.'

He paused, and began pacing up and down the small room. A flush had come into his haggard face, and his eyes were unnaturally bright. His appearance was that of a man whose emaciated body was burned up by a fever, and Peter waited in wondering silence for him to continue.

'You may think I'm exaggerating,' Jordan went on after a moment, 'and if you do I can't blame you, but I assure you I'm not. What I'm telling you is literally the truth, without frills or furbelows. Unless I can prevent it, by the twenty-seventh of July such a catastrophe will befall Great Britain as she has never

11

experienced before, a catastrophe from which it will be impossible for her to extricate herself. This plot is being engineered by a group of men of varying nationalities to whom patriotism means nothing but money everything; a group of financiers who have evolved a scheme which will make them practically the rulers of the world. And I am the only man who can prevent it!'

'These people know that, and so they have strained every nerve to ensure my silence. During the past nine years fifteen attempts have been made on my life. I thought when I landed at Southampton this morning that I had succeeded in covering my trail pretty well. The first person I saw on the quay was a man who I knew was a paid spy in the employ of this group. I don't mind admitting that the sight of him alarmed me. It had been my intention to make my way direct to Whitehall and lay my discoveries before the Government, but the sight of this man made me change my plans. I knew that if I attempted to carry out my original intention I should never have reached London alive!'

'Surely,' protested Peter, 'you would have been safe enough in broad daylight?'

A grim smile curved Norris Jordan's thin lips.

'You don't know these people, Clayton,' he said. 'They will stick at nothing to ensure the successful carrying out of their scheme, and I am their only danger. They would have taken any risks to have prevented my reaching London with the information in my possession. Whatever had happened to me, they themselves would have been immune from discovery. The people they employ are fanatics, people who are prepared and willing to sacrifice their lives for the sake of what they erroneously imagine is the cause of freedom and a better civilisation. I would have been killed openly and my murderer would have cheerfully gone to the scaffold.

'When I saw that man on the quay I realised the danger. I knew that my only hope was to elude my trailers and come to you; my flat was too dangerous, they would expect me to make for there, and another of their emissaries would have been waiting. I had kept in touch with the English papers during my travels, and I knew of your inheritance. I put through a telephone call from Southampton to the 'Daily Record' and from them obtained your address. The rest of the day I spent in trying to shake my trailer off. I think I succeeded; I hope I did.'

He glanced again at the window, and Peter had opened his mouth to put a question when he went on:

'I may come out of this alive — I hope I shall; but if I don't, Clayton, I want you to promise me that you'll follow it up. That's why I decided to come to you. I have taken certain precautions that seemed to be necessary — that in case these people should bring about my death, my labours would not be wasted. I have written down a full account of my discoveries, and these detailed notes I have divided into seven sections and each section has been sent to a friend in England in whom I have implicit trust. Each section by itself is meaningless; together they contain the whole story — all the evidence necessary to prevent this infernal conspiracy! Even the friends among whom I have distributed this evidence do not know its significance. The notes have been concealed in common objects which I have requested them to hold until I collected them personally or until somebody holding my authority should do so.'

'Rather an elaborate precaution,' remarked Peter, but Jordan shook his head.

'No precaution could be too elaborate in dealing with this group,' he answered. 'I have evidence that the majority of my letters were tampered with. If they had had an inkling of what I was doing they would have prevented my scheme at all costs.' He took his pipe from his lips and pressed the tobacco down in the bowl. 'What I want you to do, Clayton, is this,' he went on. 'If anything should happen to me between now and tomorrow night, take this immediately to Mr. Green, of Green and Hinton, Clifford's Inn.'

He took from his inside pocket a slip of paper and held it out. Peter read the scrawled words and his eyebrows went up in amazement.

'Near where Perdita's bones are laid

The Holy Ferryman plies his trade.
Obtain from him the Prior's Key
And solve this little mystery.'

'What the dickens does this mean?' he asked.

'Green will understand,' replied Jordan. 'It contains the clue to the man who holds the first of my notes. The clue to the second man is contained in them.'

'But why not — ' began Peter, and broke off with an exclamation as there came a sound from the window.

Both he and Jordan swung round, and as they did so there was a shattering crash of breaking glass, the curtains were wrenched aside, and two shots echoed deafeningly in the confined space of the tiny sitting room.

Peter caught a glimpse of a man's hand holding a smoking automatic, and then he saw Jordan stagger and crumple to the floor, the blood welling from a wound in his neck.

'Jordan!' he began anxiously, stooping over his friend, but the dying man waved him away.

'They've — got me — ' he said,

speaking thickly and with difficulty. 'I'm finished. Look after yourself, Clayton. Get — that — to — Green. Tell him — tell him — Dene of the Secret Ser . . . '

His head fell back, and before he could complete the sentence he was dead!

2

The Man Who Died

Peter was given no time to think over the sudden tragedy that had occurred. A third and a fourth shot came from the window, and he felt a sharp pain sear through his right shoulder. Springing to his feet he swung round and extinguished the lamp. A fifth bullet whistled past his ear as he did so, and a further sound of breaking glass warned him that the killers of Norris Jordan were smashing down the window, preparatory to effecting an entrance.

Noiselessly he crept to the door and ran swiftly along the little passage that led to the kitchen. His shoulder was hot where the bullet had struck him, but he felt no pain, and was thankful to find that he could use the arm. With fingers that shook in spite of his efforts to control them, he drew back the bolts of the back door and turned the key.

He had no particular plan in mind except to get away from the cottage and carry out Jordan's instructions. What had happened in the last five minutes had shown him, as nothing else could have, how desperately true every word his friend had uttered had been.

He came to the hedge that divided the cottage garden from the road, and heedless of scratches forced his way through. He heard a shout behind him and realized that one of the men had given the alarm. Pausing for a second, breathless, and in the narrow roadway, he glanced quickly about him.

A few yards beyond the gate of the cottage a red light showed dimly through the rain. It was the tail lamp of a car!

Peter's brain worked rapidly. Undoubtedly the car belonged to the people who were at that moment searching for him, and it was more than likely that it was unattended. If he could gain possession of it, here lay his means of escape. He moved forward quickly, keeping in the shadow of the hedge, and presently came to within a yard of the stationary machine. His heart leaped as he saw that the driving-seat was empty.

Never so long as he lived did Peter forget that wild midnight ride. The numbness of his wound, which had prevented him feeling any pain, wore off, and presently his shoulder began to throb with a dull ache that seemed to spread all over his body.

It came to him with something of a shock that the danger that had threatened his friend was now transferred to him. These people, whose schemes Jordan had discovered, would be under the impression that he had passed on his information to Peter and, in consequence, would transfer their murderous attention to him. It was anything but a pleasant outlook.

Remembering the meaningless rhyme that Jordan had given him, Peter felt in his pocket for it, but failed to find it. A more careful examination proved that it was no longer in his possession. Wrinkling his forehead he strove to remember exactly what he had done with it. He had been holding it in his hand when Jordan had been shot. In the paralyzing shock he had experienced at that precise moment he must have dropped it, though luckily he could remember the wording:

'Near where Perdita's bones are laid
The Holy Ferryman plies his trade.
Obtain from him the Prior's Key
And solve this little mystery.'

That was it, and Jordan had said that Green would understand. The gleam in his eyes manifested his grim determination. His arm was hurting him considerably and he decided that at the first opportunity he would have it attended to by a doctor. It would be wise to do that at once. He had several hours to fill in somehow before it would be possible to seek out Green; the address Jordan had given him was obviously an office one, and therefore the man was unlikely to arrive before half past nine at the earliest, and it was now only a little after four.

Peter drove slowly through the deserted expanse of Knightsbridge, and presently saw what he was seeking, the red lamp which marks a doctor's house. The sleepy-eyed man who came in answer to his ring at the night-bell stared in astonishment when he explained his injury

'Come into the surgery,' he said, and made an examination. 'I'm afraid this is going to hurt a bit,' he remarked after he had inspected the wound. 'The bullet has lodged in the muscle. How in the world did you manage to do it?'

Peter explained glibly that he had been cleaning a revolver and had accidentally pressed the trigger. The doctor obviously disbelieved him, but he said nothing, and set about extracting the bullet. It was a painful operation, and left him white and shaky, but when his shoulder had been dressed it certainly felt a little easier.

'You're lucky,' remarked the doctor, 'that it wasn't worse. It only just missed smashing your shoulder blade by an inch!'

He pocketed the fee which Peter paid him, and accompanied his patient to the door.

The rain had ceased, and there were indications that the coming day would be a fine one. It occurred to Peter, as he drove slowly along Piccadilly, that the car might contain some clue to the identity of the people responsible for Jordan's death. Turning into a side street he brought it to a halt and made an examination. But there was nothing to suggest to whom it belonged. The registration number might supply this information but of this he was doubtful. He was beginning to feel hungry, and stopped at a Lyons' Corner House for breakfast.

By the time he had finished the meal and smoked several cigarettes it was nearly nine o'clock, and he decided to set forth for the offices of Green and Hinton in Clifford's Inn. He reached that respectable neighbourhood as a nearby clock chimed the quarter past.

A search of the various plates on the lintels of the old-fashioned houses showed that Green and Hinton were a firm of solicitors. Nobody had apparently arrived yet, for the outer door was closed, so Peter waited. He hadn't very long to wait, for presently a man in the conventional black of a lawyer's clerk arrived and let himself in with a key. Giving him a few minutes, Peter followed and entered the outer office. The man he had seen arrive came forward to greet him.

'I want to see Mr. Green,' said Peter. 'I have an important message for him from Mr. Norris Jordan.'

'I know Mr. Jordan, sir,' replied the clerk, 'but I'm afraid you can't see Mr. Green.'

'Why not?' asked Peter. 'If he hasn't come yet, I'll wait.'

'It isn't a question of waiting, sir,' answered the clerk. 'You see, Mr. Green died yesterday!'

3

Dene of the Secret Service

Peter stared at the man incredulously. 'Mr. Green died yesterday?' he stammered.

The grey-haired clerk nodded gravely.

'Yes, sir,' he replied. 'For a long time Mr. Green has suffered from heart trouble, and yesterday morning he had an attack which, unfortunately, proved fatal.'

Peter's heart sank. Jordan had said that Green would understand the message. But Green was dead!

'Is there anyone else I can see?' he enquired. 'The matter is urgent.'

The clerk shook his head.

'There's only me, sir,' he said. 'I'm carrying on the business for a few days until the executors of the will decide what shall be done. Mr. Green was a widower without children, and I presume, although I could not say for certain, that our clientele will be transferred to another firm.'

Peter considered his next move, and found it difficult to make up his mind. Obviously it was useless taking the clerk into his confidence, it was unlikely that he would know anything concerning Jordan's private affairs or be in a position to elucidate the meaning of the rhyme. A few careful questions confirmed him in this opinion, and reluctantly he took his leave.

What was it that Jordan had said before death had silenced him for ever? Something about Dene, Dene of the Secret Ser ... That could only mean the Secret Service. Naturally the business on which Jordan had been engaged would come under the auspices of the Secret Service. That ought to be fairly easy, he concluded. The Foreign Office would be able to help him there. The best thing he could do would be to find this man Dene at once and tell him the whole story

The finding of Dene was not as easy as he had anticipated. The fact that Great Britain possesses a Secret Service at all is treated as a polite fiction by the Powers that Be. The Foreign Official to whom he put his enquiry looked a little vague and passed him on to another and equally evasive gentleman, who murmured something about it not being that department, and sent him in search of someone else.

Eventually he interviewed an under-secretary who seemed to possess a little more intelligence than the others.

They went up in a lift, passed down a long corridor, and stopped outside a polished rosewood door. His guide tapped, turned the handle, and opening the door, stood aside for Peter to enter.

He found himself in a large, comfortably furnished office. A thick pile carpet covered the floor, and the walls were surrounded with bookshelves. In the centre was a big, flat-topped desk littered with papers, behind which, with his back to the light, sat a lean-faced man with a high forehead and keen, grey eyes.

'Sit down, Mr. Clayton,' he said, as Peter stood hesitating. 'You say in your note that you want to see me on urgent business connected with the safety of Great Britain, and that you've come on behalf of Mr. Norris Jordan.'

Peter nodded and sank into the deep leather chair in front of the desk.

'On an average,' said the grey-eyed man, 'we have about fifty people a day coming here making the same assertion. It was only because I knew Norris Jordan some years ago that I attached more importance to this note of yours than to the others.'

Peter understood why it had been so difficult to gain his interview with this man.

Without further preamble he began his story, and Dene, leaning back in his chair, his fingertips pressed together, his eyes half closed, listened intently.

'It seems,' he remarked, when Peter had concluded, 'that you're a very lucky man, Mr. Clayton. I have no doubt that these people would have killed you, too, if you had not succeeded in making your escape.'

'I've no doubt, either,' said Peter grimly.

'I don't mind telling you,' Dene continued, 'that we have heard rumours of some such conspiracy as poor Jordan mentioned, but up till now we have not been able to find anything to substantiate them. You say he told you that the matter was to come to a head on July the twenty-seventh.'

'Yes,' replied Peter.

Dene picked up the large calendar on his desk and consulted it.

'It is now the twenty-seventh of June,' he murmured. 'That gives us thirty days, thirty days to find these people to whom Jordan entrusted the results of his discovery. He gave you no inkling as to the nature of this plot?'

Peter shook his head.

'None,' he answered.

The level brows of the man behind the desk drew together in a frown.

'It's a thousand pities that this Mr. Green should have died,' he muttered, 'for apparently he alone knew the secret of that rhyme. However, it can't be helped, and we must do our best to solve it for ourselves. Would you mind repeating it again?'

He picked up a pencil and drew a pad of paper towards him and Peter complied.

'You're sure,' said Dene, when he had written it down, 'that you've got this correct?'

'Quite sure,' said Peter. 'It's not very difficult to remember.'

Now that he had told his story he was feeling a little easier in his mind. Dene's reception of it had been better than he had expected.

'Of course you realize,' said the grey-eyed man, eyeing him keenly, 'that from now on you yourself will be in considerable danger. These people will guess that Jordan passed on a certain amount, if not all the result of his discoveries to you.'

'I am aware of that!' retorted Peter a little grimly, and the other smiled.

'It's fairly obvious I think,' he said, 'but maybe we shall be able to use it to our advantage. One moment, Mr. Clayton, I want to think something out.'

So suddenly, that Peter was a little startled, the dreamy introspective attitude of the man before him changed to one of alert activity. Leaning forward abruptly he picked up the telephone and gave a number. 'This is Dene speaking,' he said when he was connected, 'of K department, Special Branch. Ask Inspector Dilly to come over to me at once.'

He hung up the receiver took a battered pipe from the tray on the desk in front of him and began to fill it from a large tobacco jar near his elbow.

'You say the car,' he said abruptly as though there had been no break in his questioning, 'in which you succeeded in escaping is outside. Can you remember the number?'

'XN 4409,' answered Peter promptly.

Dene pressed a button on his desk, struck a match, and puffed at his pipe. Almost immediately in answer to his summons a man came quietly into the office.

'I want to trace the owner of a car, registered number XN 4409,' said Dene, scribbling the number on a memo pad and tearing off the sheet. 'Get what information you can and let me have it at once.'

'Yes, sir.' The man took the paper and noiselessly made his exit.

When he had gone Dene began to ply Peter with questions. Point by point he took him through his story again, elaborating every detail, and Peter had an uneasy feeling at the back of his mind that he was seeking for a discrepancy.

'Now,' he said, when he had finished, 'I think I've got the whole thing pretty clear. Of course I shall have to go down to your cottage, there's just the possibility that these people may have left some clue behind, which will enable me to trace them.'

He broke off as there came a tap at the door and the man who had ushered Peter in entered.

'Inspector Dilly, sir.' he said.

'Come in, Dilly,' called Dene, and a tall, seedily dressed individual came slouching across the threshold.

He was the thinnest man Peter had ever seen, and his stained mackintosh and worn derby hat made him look like an out-of-work commercial traveller.

'You sent for me, Mr. Dene?' he enquired in a lugubrious voice.

Dene nodded.

'Yes, Dilly.' he answered. 'This is Mr. Clayton, of Briar Cottage, near Lethways. A man called Norris Jordan was murdered in his cottage last night and I want you to arrest Mr. Clayton for the crime!'

4

The Missing Rhyme

Peter's stomach went through a peculiarly unpleasant performance. So his story had not been believed. This man with the keen grey eyes who had listened so intently had merely been playing with him, had pretended to accept what he had said in order to keep him there while he sent for the police.

'I suppose you think that's smart!' he said angrily. 'But I call it a mean trick! If you didn't believe me why couldn't you have said so? I came here of my own free will and everything I have said has been the truth. If you were under the impression — '

'One moment! One moment, Mr. Clayton — ' interrupted Michael Dene smoothly. 'I haven't said that I don't believe you.'

'You haven't said it in so many words!'

snapped Peter, his face red with anger. 'But having me arrested is proof enough, I should think.'

A faint smile curved Dene's lips and his eyes twinkled.

'I'm afraid you're under a misapprehension,' he said. 'If you will give me a chance and listen I will explain. Sit down, Inspector.' He turned to the thin detective. 'This is for your benefit as well as Mr. Clayton's.'

Inspector Dilly perched himself uncomfortably on the extreme edge of the chair and Michael Dene went on.

'I am prepared to believe every word of your story, but there is no reason why we should not try to hoodwink the people at the back of this conspiracy. If they are as clever as I think them to be and as Jordan evidently knew them to be, they will know by now that you have been to see me. If it becomes public that you have been arrested for Jordan's murder they will be under the impression that your story has been disbelieved and we shall kill two birds with one stone: we shall lull them into a false impression of security and also save you from suffering the same fate as poor Jordan.'

Peter understood.

'I — I'm sorry,' he muttered, 'but I thought — '

'My suggestion is this,' Dene continued, acknowledging the interruption with a nod. 'Inspector Dilly will escort you from here and take you to Scotland Yard, where you will be formally charged with the murder of Norris Jordan. Anyone who may be watching your movements will be satisfied that you have been arrested for the crime. A paragraph will be sent to the newspapers to that effect. At Scotland Yard your appearance will be changed so that when you leave that building you will be unrecognisable as Peter Clayton. So far as the public, and these people we are up against are concerned, Peter Clayton will be languishing in his cell awaiting his trial. Under your new identity — you can adopt any name you like — you will be of immense assistance to me in running these people to earth. You see the advantage of the scheme?'

Peter not only saw but said so. He was

so relieved to find that his arrest was merely a matter of form that he would have agreed to anything, and the fact that he was allowed to take a hand against the unknown people who had been responsible for the murder of Jordan was only what he could have wished for.

'While your appearance is being altered,' said Dene, 'I will get in touch with the Chief Constable of Berkshire and inform him that the murder of Jordan is of political importance and a matter for the Special Branch. That will keep the local police from doing anything until I arrive. It shouldn't take longer than an hour for your exchange of identity, and if you come back here you can go down with me to your cottage as my assistant.'

When he was once more admitted to Michael Dene's office he found the Secret Service man waiting, his hat and coat on, ready to depart. He glanced keenly at Peter, taking in his new appearance with one quick, comprehensive stare.

'You'll do!' he said briefly, 'I've found a name for you that will fit your new appearance. From now on I shall call you

Harry Pinner, don't forget that.'

A big car was waiting for them downstairs and Dene took the wheel, with Peter beside him.

As they turned into the narrow road that led past Peter's gate he saw a car standing by the hedge and noted signs of activity in the region of the cottage. A uniformed constable was on guard near the porch and a thick-set man, wearing the peaked cap of an inspector, was examining the broken windows of the sitting room. He interrupted his occupation to come forward as Dene and Peter walked up the little path.

'Are you Mr. Dene?' he asked, and when Dene nodded: 'I'm Inspector Fledgley, sir. The Chief Constable warned me that you'd be coming and asked me to apologize that he couldn't wait to see you himself. This is a nasty business, sir, and it's pretty obvious who shot this fellow. A man called Clayton is the occupant of this cottage and he's missing.'

'He's at present safely confined in Scotland Yard,' answered Dene, and the inspector's rather prominent eyes bulged.

'Is he now!' he exclaimed. 'Well, that's pretty smart work. 'Ow did they come to get 'im so quickly?'

'It's a long story and I'm afraid I haven't time to tell you, Inspector,' answered Dene smoothly, 'and no doubt your Chief Constable has informed you that there's more in this matter than appears on the surface?'

The inspector, who was a great reader of sensational literature in his spare moments, nodded gravely.

'So I was told, sir,' he said. 'Something political, I understood. I suppose this feller Clayton was a foreign spy or somethin'?'

'He is one of the most dangerous men in England,' agreed Dene seriously. 'By the way, Inspector, this is my assistant, Mr. Pinner. We should like to have a look round. I suppose nothing has been touched?'

Fledgley shook his head.

'No, sir, nothin',' he answered. 'The first person to give the alarm was Mrs. Rodgers, a woman what lives in the village who comes up every day to do the cleanin'. She arrived as usual and found the place in a shockin' state, and this feller lyin' dead in the middle of the sittin' room. We 'aven't been able to identify him yet. But maybe you can 'elp us, sir?'

'The man's name is Jordan — Norris Jordan,' answered Dene, and the inspector noted down his reply in a bulky notebook.

They passed into the cottage, and Peter looked round at the little home he had so recently left and gasped inwardly. His usually neat abode looked as if a cyclone had struck it. The coats hanging in the hallstand had had their pockets turned inside out and been thrown hastily down. An oak chest in which he kept brown paper and string and other odds and ends was open, its contents strewn over the polished floor.

Michael Dene stood for a moment just inside the door and allowed his keen eyes to travel quickly round the room. There was evidence here that a thorough search had been made. A small bureau in the corner had been denuded of its drawers and the papers they had contained were scattered in all directions. The books had been torn from the bookshelves and flung down and the pockets of the dead man turned inside out.

'I shouldn't take too much notice of the state of the place sir,' said Inspector Fledgley. 'In my opinion it's all a bluff. This feller — Jordan you say his name is — came to see Clayton: they quarrelled, Clayton shot him and then tried to make it look, by smashing the window and scattering all these things about, as though somebody had broken in from outside. That's my theory, sir.'

'I shouldn't be at all surprised,' murmured Dene absently.

He stooped and turned the body gently over, peering at the floor beneath. Peter guessed that he was searching for the original of the rhyme which he had had in his hand at the time Jordan was shot, and his guess was confirmed when, the inspector leaving them for a moment, Dene turned towards him. 'Make a thorough search and see if you can find that scrap of paper,' he murmured. 'I don't think you will, but we must make certain. If you don't find it then the murderers of Jordan took it away with them, which means we've got to beat

41

them to its solution.'

Peter made a careful search, but the paper was nowhere to be found.

'I didn't expect it would be here,' said Dene, frowning, when Peter told him. 'We couldn't hope that they would overlook that. Let's see if we can find anything that will help us outside.'

They went out into the bright sunlight, and the Secret Service man made a careful examination of the gravel beneath the window. Several footprints were visible, but for the most part they could be identified as having been made by the large boots of Inspector Fledgley, and Dene clicked his teeth impatiently.

'Whatever traces there might have been have been destroyed,' he said. 'Well, there's nothing more to be done here; we'll go back to my office and tackle that rhyme. That's our trump card. If we can solve that and find these seven people to whom Norris Jordan entrusted the evidence he had collected before the twenty-seventh of July, and before this group forestall us, we shall have the game in our hands.'

5

The First Clue

They reached London in time for a late lunch and over the meal arrangements were fixed up for Peter's immediate future. It was obvious that he could no longer occupy the Berkshire cottage, and therefore other accommodation had to be found. At Dene's suggestion he decided to book a room at one of the small hotels that abound in the Victoria district. It was within easy reach of Whitehall and the clients of such hostelries consisted mostly of travellers and birds of passage who came and went at frequent intervals, so that Peter's arrival would pass unnoticed among the rest.

When this had been decided upon, the question of money arose. When he had left the little cottage Peter had had in his possession a little over eighteen shillings, and he had brought with him neither cheque book nor any means of obtaining a further supply. It was impossible for him to visit his bank, for the early editions of the newspapers already carried an account of the murder and the news of Peter's arrest. It was Michael Dene who found a solution to the problem.

'Tell me the name of your bank,' he said, 'and I'll arrange to get hold of a cheque form. You can fill in the cheque for the amount you want, making it payable to me and dating it three days back. I'll give you cash in return, and pass it through my bank in the ordinary way. Your bank will then only imagine that it was drawn before your arrest.'

This plan was put into execution immediately after they had finished lunch. Peter went off and secured a room in a quiet hotel in Victoria Station, bought several things that he needed, and returned to Dene's office, to find him deep in the problem of the rhyme.

'I think,' he said, when Peter had drawn up a chair to the desk and lighted a cigarette, 'that we can take it for granted that all these people mentioned by Jordan reside in England.'

Peter nodded.

'Yes, he said that,' he answered.

'And this holds the clue to number one,' Michael Dene went on, 'though at the moment I must confess I can't see how.' He had a copy of the rhyme before him on the desk and read it over aloud,

'Near where Perdita's bones are laid,
The Holy Ferryman plies his trade.
Obtain from him the Prior's Key,
And solve this little mystery.'

'Obviously the clue we want lies in the first two lines. The Prior's Key is the thing we've got to ask for when we find out who the Holy Ferryman is.'

'And that's not going to be so easy,' interjected Peter with a grimace.

'No,' answered Dene frowning, 'but it's by no means impossible. The first thing we have to do is to discover who Perdita is, or rather was.'

He got up, went over to the rows of bookshelves that lined the office and took down a volume of the 'Encyclopaedia Britannica.'

'Here we are,' he said. 'Perdita was

Mrs. Mary Robinson, portraits of whom, by three of the greatest masters of the art, Gainsborough, Reynolds, and Romney, may be seen in the Wallace collection, London.'

'Near where Perdita's bones are laid!' said Peter excitedly. 'That must mean where she was buried.' Dene nodded.

'Yes,' he answered. 'And she was buried in the village churchyard at Old Windsor in the Staines Road.'

'It's easy!' exclaimed Peter.

'Don't be too optimistic,' warned Michael Dene, as he closed the volume and laid it aside. 'We have yet to find the Holy Ferryman.'

'That shouldn't be difficult now,' said Peter. ' 'Near where Perdita's bones are laid' . . . that means he's somewhere in the vicinity.'

'All the same,' answered the other, 'we've still got to find him, Pinner.'

Peter grinned as he heard his new name.

'I think our next course is a visit to Old Windsor and see if we can't locate this peculiar person.'

They reached the village of Old Windsor, that ancient seat of Saxon Kings, a little after six o'clock and Dene suggested a drink.

'We'll go along to the Bells of Ouseley,' he said. 'It's a pretty place on the river bank and a popular resort of artists, anglers and river loungers, and maybe we shall be able to pick up something concerning the objects of our search.'

Passing through the village they drew up beside the picturesque old building whose white front is such a conspicuous feature of the river in this neighbourhood, and entering the bar ordered beer. From here they were able to look across the wide road to the river, with Claybury on the Buckinghamshire side, and Peter was just setting down his tankard after a long drink when Dene nudged his arm.

'Look there,' said the Secret Service man, and his eyes glinted.

Peter followed the direction of his gaze and saw, coming slowly across the broad expanse of the river, a ferryboat. It contained several people, and was being propelled steadily towards the landing stage, which belonged to the inn. But it was neither the boat nor the passengers that caused him to draw in his breath quickly and glance at the man at his side — it was the rower! He was a clergyman, a stoutish, jovial looking man, whose bald head gleamed in the sunlight and whose clerical collar was unmistakable.

'The Holy Ferryman!' breathed Peter, and Dene nodded.

'That's rather unusual,' he remarked to the girl behind the bar, and jerked his head towards the ferry. 'It's not often you see a parson acting as ferryman.'

The barmaid smiled.

'You must be a stranger in this neighbourhood,' she answered, 'Otherwise you wouldn't be surprised. That's the Reverend Colgate-Jones. He's the Vicar of Claybury, and the vicarage is on the riverbank. When he's not otherwise engaged he works the ferry.'

The ferryboat came slowly in, was skilfully brought up to the landing stage, and the half dozen passengers alighted.

'Are you going to tackle him now?' asked Peter below his breath. And Dene nodded.

'Might as well,' he said. 'The quicker

we get hold of the Prior's Key the better. Don't forget the group we're up against is also in possession of the clue, and if we found it easy to solve they probably found it just as easy.'

He drained his tankard, set it down and, leaving the inn, crossed the road and made his way to the waterside with Peter at his heels. The Reverend Colgate-Jones was in the act of preparing to return to the other side.

'Will you take us across?' enquired Michael Dene pleasantly.

'With the greatest of pleasure, sir,' said the clergyman and they stepped down into the flat-bottomed ferry.

'A lovely afternoon, is it not?' he remarked, as they moved slowly over the water. 'Quite a delightful change, after the past two or three days.'

Dene agreed.

'Am I right in supposing,' he said, 'that you are Mr. Colgate-Jones?'

The clergyman nodded.

'You're quite right,' he replied. 'Though I'm afraid you have the advantage of me. Have I met you before, sir?'

'No,' said Michael Dene. 'But I think you were acquainted with a friend of mine — a Mr. Norris Jordan.'

The small, bright, brown eyes gave him a keen glance.

'I was a great friend of Jordan's,' answered the clergyman gravely. 'Norris Jordan and I went to school together. May I ask if you are connected with the police?'

'Why should you imagine that?' asked Dene.

'Because,' said Mr. Jones, 'I have just read an account of poor Jordan's tragic end, and I wondered whether — whether perhaps you might be.'

'No, we are not connected with the police,' said Dene truthfully, 'although I may as well candidly admit that our object in coming here this afternoon was to seek you out.'

The clergyman made no reply, but an alert look came into his eyes, and there was a question behind it,

'I believe,' Dene went on, 'that some years ago Norris Jordan sent you an object, with instructions to keep it until such time as he should call for it personally or should send someone with his authority to collect it.'

'You may be correct,' said the Reverend Colgate-Jones. 'On the other hand you may not. Unless you can inform me what this object is you mention, I'm afraid I can't tell you.'

'The Prior's Key!' said Dene; and the stout clergyman's face cleared.

'I should be glad if you would come to the vicarage,' he said. 'We shall be across shortly, and I can discuss the matter better in the privacy of my study.'

'With pleasure,' agreed the Secret Service man.

The ferry was brought in to a wooden landing stage, and they disembarked. Waiting while the stout clergyman made the boat fast they followed him up a sloping lawn, through a garden gay with flowers and into the coolness of an old-fashioned gabled house that stood a hundred yards or so back from the river's bank. He led the way into a lofty, untidy room and waved them to a couple of deep chairs.

'Sit down, gentlemen,' he said. 'If you

would care for a drink please help your-selves.' He indicated a table on which stood a tray with whisky, soda and glasses.

'Thank you,' said Dene. 'Perhaps before we go any further, Mr. Jones, I had better introduce myself. My name is Michael Dene and I am connected with the Special Branch of the Foreign Office Intelligence Department. This is my assistant, Mr. Pinner.'

Their host acknowledged the introduc-tion with a short bow, and sank into a padded chair behind a littered writing table.

'So you've come for the Prior's Key?' he said softly, looking from one to the other. 'Well, I suppose I'd better give it to you.'

He unlocked a drawer in the desk, rum-maged among its contents and brought to light a large, curiously shaped key, made from some metal that looked like bronze.

'There it is, gentlemen,' he said, holding it out in his palm. 'And if you can tell me, without divulging any State Secret, what its significance is, I shall be very pleased. I must confess that I am very curious.'

6

The Secret of the Prior's Key

Michael Dene took the key from the clergyman's hand and examined it. It was obviously very old and rather heavy; the wards were of an unusual shape and the handle was in the form of a cross. As a curio it appeared to him to be unique. He mentioned this to Colgate-Jones and the vicar agreed with him.

'I have never seen anything like it before,' he declared. 'It appears to be of ancient German manufacture, which is borne out by the fact that poor Jordan sent it to me from Leipzig.'

'When did you receive it?' inquired Dene, squinting down the barrel.

'On April the fifth,' answered Colgate-Jones.

'Have you, by any chance, the letter that accompanied it?' inquired the Secret Service man.

The clergyman hesitated.

'I have,' he replied, 'but I should like to know more about this business before I show it to you. I'm not doubting your word, Mr. Dene, that you're connected with the Special Branch of the Foreign Office, but I have no proof. In handing over the key I am merely carrying out my poor friend's instructions, but beyond that I do not feel inclined to go, in the very peculiar circumstances surrounding his death, unless you can supply me with a little more information.'

'That will prove my credentials,' Dene said, handing over a document.

The Reverend Colgate-Jones glanced at the world famous signature with which it was signed, and nodded in complete satisfaction.

'You will forgive me for being cautious, Mr. Dene,' he said passing it back, 'but you can understand, it is only natural after the tragic way in which Jordan met his death.' Searching among the contents of the drawer from which he had taken the key he produced a letter. 'Here is the letter which accompanied the key,' he said, and pushed it across the writing table.

Dene read the short note, which ran as follows:

Leipzig, April 2nd.
My Dear Jones,
No doubt you will be surprised to hear from me after such a long silence, but I picked up the enclosed curio in a small shop in Leipzig and feel sure it will interest you. It is called the Prior's Key and is, I believe, very old. Keep it carefully for me until I either come and claim it personally or send someone who will ask for it.
Always sincerely yours,
Norris J.

'It is quite an innocuous letter, as you will observe,' said the clergyman, 'and contains no explanation regarding the significance of the key whatever.'

'I have told you all I know concerning this business,' said Dene, 'because I believe you may be in a position to help us. According to what Jordan told

Clayton he had written a detailed account of his discoveries and sent it in seven sections to seven of his friends. You are obviously one of them, and may be able to supply me with the names and addresses of the others.'

The clergyman shook his head.

'I'm afraid I can't, Mr. Dene,' he said. 'I knew none of Jordan's friends, with the exception of Green. He was a reticent man and spoke very little about himself.'

Michael Dene was disappointed,

'In that case,' he said, 'we shall have to rely on our ability to follow the clues which he has left.'

'I know of someone else,' said Colgate-Jones thoughtfully, 'who might be of assistance. That is Jordan's sister. She telephoned, poor girl, immediately she heard of her brother's death, and I suggested that she should come down here for a few days. If you and — er — and Mr. Clayton,' — Dene had told him of Peter's real identity — 'would care to stop for dinner I should be happy to introduce you.'

'That's very kind of you,' said Michael

Dene. 'I shall be very pleased to accept your invitation. Now, let's see if we can solve the secret of the key.' He picked it up. 'It should contain,' he went on, 'one section of Jordan's notes and the clue to the person who holds another. The most obvious place, of course, is inside the barrel, and I notice that a little way from the end it has been stopped with some substance or other. Have you a pin?'

Colgate-Jones reached towards a tray containing a collection of oddments and produced the article required. Dene began to probe in the end of the key carefully, and after a little while succeeded in extracting a gummy substance. Tapping the key on the desk to clear it of this he looked once more down the barrel and caught a glimpse of something white.

'There is a rolled up paper here,' he announced.

Glancing quickly about him he picked up a pipe lighter, and with its assistance, after a little trouble, was able to withdraw a thin roll of paper. Spreading it out flat he discovered that it was a narrow strip cut from a quarto sheet of very thin typing paper. At the top was the figure one, and below a series of written words, some of them half complete. Peter and the Reverend Colgate-Jones had risen and come to his side. Peering over his shoulder they read the disconnected words:

1.
In c . . .
the
years.
which
The pe . . .
men
They
inventi . . .
their
reserve,
it at
the eve . . .
For fi . . .
gold
a pl . . .
have
and
to co . . .

The n . . .
Paul
Wu L
The o . . .
The
July
Buckin . . .
evide . . .
this
being

'I'm afraid it supplies us with little information,' murmured Dene. 'What Jordan did, evidently, was to write the whole thing out on a quarto sheet of paper and then cut it up into seven strips. Until we've got them all, or nearly all, and can fit them together again we shall be unable to make sense.'

He turned the strip of paper over and discovered that a rhyme had been written on the back, a similar rhyme to that which Jordan had given Peter just before his death.

'A key suggests to the mind
A lock — and it's not hard to find.
A child will help, so seek one out,

And keep, ergo, free from doubt.'

'Clue number two,' said Dene frowning. 'And if we can solve that it should lead us to the person who has in his possession the second section of the document we've got to piece together before July the twenty-seventh.'

7

Men of the Night

The Reverend Colgate-Jones' establishment was a bachelor one, presided over by an efficient housekeeper. The dinner she provided was excellent, and both Michael Dene and Peter thoroughly enjoyed the meal in the cool, airy dining room.

'You have no idea of the nature of this plot, I presume?' asked their host, when the sweet had been served.

Dene shook his head.

'No idea at all,' he declared. 'For a long time rumours have trickled into my department concerning the fact that something was brewing, but we have been unable to pin them down to anything more than rumours.'

'I've been thinking over that clue,' said Colgate-Jones, 'and although I'm pretty good at puzzles I must confess it's beaten me.'

'It's beaten me, too,' admitted Dene, 'for the present at any rate. It's more difficult than the one that led us to you. That was comparatively easy — which reminds me, by the way, that our unknown enemies are in possession of it, and it's quite possible they may turn up at any moment.'

The round, cheery face of their host set grimly,

'I wish they would!' he declared. 'I should like to have the opportunity of tackling them.'

Dene had opened his mouth to reply when there came a tap at the door and the housekeeper entered.

'Miss Jordan has arrived, sir,' she said, and Colgate-Jones got heavily to his feet. 'Ask her to come in,' he said, and greeted the girl who presently entered with outstretched hands.

'Sit down, my dear,' he said. 'We didn't wait dinner for you, but if there's anything you would like tell Mrs. Sutherland.'

'I don't want anything, thank you,' said Mary Jordan, sinking into the chair that he pulled forward for her. 'Is — isn't this dreadful — about Norris?'

'Yes. I'm very, very sorry,' said Colgate-Jones, and he infused into the words a sympathy that could not have been conveyed better in the most elaborate sentence. 'Don't think about it more than you can help.'

Norris Jordan's sister was a surprise to Peter. He had never met her before, and he had expected someone much older. He put her age in the region of twenty-six, and learned later that he was a year out in his reckoning. Slim and fair-haired, the only feature in which she resembled her brother was her eyes — they were the same deep grey.

Colgate-Jones introduced them, referring to Peter as Mr. Pinner. Michael Dene had requested that Mary Jordan should not be told the true reason for their presence, and the clergyman had agreed.

'I can scarcely realize that it's really true,' she said later, as she sipped the coffee that Colgate-Jones handed to her. 'That Norris is — is dead, I mean. Why do you think he was murdered, Uncle?'

'That is a difficult question to answer, my dear,' replied the vicar. 'The police will know more about that than I.'

'Were you acquainted with any of your brother's friends?' asked Michael Dene.

She shook her head.

'Very few,' she answered. 'I've heard him speak of this horrible man, Clayton,' — Peter squirmed uneasily — 'and one or two of his Fleet Sheet acquaintances, but I don't know any of the others.'

'You know me,' said Colgate-Jones with a smile.

She looked it him affectionately.

'I've known you since I was a little girl,' she answered. 'I look upon you more as a relation than a friend.'

So skilfully that the girl failed to realize that she was being questioned, Dene took charge of the conversation, and extracted all the information she was able to give, and it was very little. Obviously she knew nothing that was likely to help them in their search.

The weather had changed while they had been talking. Heavy copper-tinged clouds obscured the sky, and the first low rumble of the threatened storm reached their ears as Dene rose to take his departure.

'I'm afraid we shall have a wet run back,' he remarked

'Why go?' suggested Colgate-Jones. 'I can easily put you up. There's no reason, unless you have some pressing business to attend to, why you should risk an unpleasant journey. It looks to me as if we're in for a pretty bad storm.'

A jagged ribbon of blue flame shot across the sky as he spoke, and the rumble of the thunder that followed it was louder than the previous peal.

'I don't want to put you to any inconvenience,' murmured Dene, but the clergyman cut him short.

'It's no inconvenience at all,' he declared. 'In fact, I shall be very pleased if you stay.'

It was not the conventional utterance that is usual to these occasions. Michael Dene knew that he meant what he said and guessed the reason. His calling had forced him to lead a more or less humdrum existence, and the love of adventure, which is every man's birthright, had been given no chance of expression. Now that the chance had come his way he was loath to let it go. After only a momentary hesitation the Secret Service man accepted.

'I'll have to garage the car somewhere,' he remarked

'They'll put it up at the Bells,' said the vicar, and Peter offered to row over and attend to it.

He got back just as the storm burst in full fury. The lightning and thunder were incessant, and the rain fell in sheets of water that beat down the flowers in the garden and reduced the trim gravel paths to so many miniature rivers.

'It's lucky you decided to stop,' remarked the clergyman and Dene heartily agreed with him.

When they eventually retired for the night they had made no headway. The storm was still faintly audible, and it was raining, but not so violently, as Dene took a last look through the window of his bedroom before turning in.

It was some little time before he fell

asleep. The words of the verse, which Jordan had written ran ceaselessly through his mind as he vainly tried to find a solution. Eventually, however, he dropped off into a troubled doze, from which he awoke with a start, and a conviction that something was wrong. What it was that had awakened him so suddenly he was unable to tell.

In an instant he was alert and watchful. Slipping out of bed he crossed stealthily to the window, noiselessly drew aside the curtain, and leaned out of the open casement. The night was very dark, and at first he could see nothing; and then, as his eyes grew accustomed to the gloom, he made out dimly the shadowy figures of three men standing in the garden beneath.

8

Gas!

Michael Dene held his breath and looked down at the vague forms of the men below. There was no need to ask himself who they were or why they had come — that was obvious. They were the agents of the group who had been responsible for the killing of Jordan, and the reason for their presence was the Prior's Key.

They, too, had succeeded in solving the problem of the rhyme that Peter had dropped before his flight from the cottage in Berkshire, and they had come post-haste to discover whatever evidence that key might contain against them.

Even as the Secret Service man watched, a fourth man joined the others and there was a whispered colloquy. Dene strained his ears, but he could hear nothing of what was being said. Presently, however, they all began to move stealthily away, and disappeared round an angle of the house.

He drew in his head from the window and thought rapidly. Here was an unexpected chance that might be turned to his advantage.

Hastily he pulled on a pair of trousers over his pyjamas, thrust his feet into slippers, and crossing noiselessly to the door opened it and stepped out into the darkened passage.

The room that had been allotted to Peter Clayton was next to his own; and grasping the handle he breathed a fervent hope that the door would not be locked. As it turned out it was not, and he slipped into the room.

The sound of regular breathing gave him the direction of the bed, and, moving over to it he bent down, felt for and found the sleeper's shoulder, and gently shook him. Peter woke with a start.

'Keep quiet!' whispered Dene, before he could utter a sound. 'It's I, Michael Dene.'

Briefly he explained what he had seen as the other struggled to a sitting position.

'Slip on something as quickly as you can, and wait for me here,' Dene continued in the same low whisper. 'I'm going to wake Colgate-Jones.'

He made his way to his host's bedroom door and discovered to his annoyance that it was locked. Raising his hand he tapped softly, hut there was no answer and he tapped again. He heard the creak of a mattress and a muffled voice called: 'Who's there?'

'Open the door,' said Dene as loudly as he dared. 'It's Dene.'

The bed creaked again, there was a soft padding of bare feet, the click of the key, and the door was pulled open.

'What's the matter?' asked Colgate-Jones.

'Our friends are after the key,' whispered Dene. 'There are four of them outside the house at this moment, and I don't think it will be very long before they are inside.'

He heard the vicar draw his breath sharply.

'What do you suggest we do?' he asked.

'See if we can't take them by surprise,'

said Dene. 'They're probably under the impression that they have only you to deal with. They can't very well know that Clayton and I are here. My suggestion is that the three of us wait for them to break in and see if we can bag the whole lot.'

'I'm with you,' said Colgate-Jones, and there was a note of sheer delight in his voice. 'Give me a moment while I slip on some clothes.'

The Secret Service man led the way to the head of the staircase and found Peter already waiting. The steady ticking of the clock was still the only sound that disturbed the peace of the house as they made their way softly to the hall below.

'They're almost certain to make for the study first,' said Michael Dene below his breath.

The door of the big room was partly open, and pushing it wide he stepped across the threshold. The position of the French windows showed a slightly paler oblong in the darkness.

Taking their places in a corner of the room near the big desk, they waited, and their vigil was of short duration. Quite suddenly the stillness was broken by a faint creaking sound.

Slowly the door began to swing open, there was a click and a fan-shaped ray of light began to play about the darkened room. In the faint reflection of the beam Dene saw that the torch was held in the hand of a man dressed entirely in black, whose face was covered by something of the same hue. Behind the first intruder he could dimly make out the shadowy figure of a second man.

It was Peter who unconsciously brought about the disaster that followed. The floor of the study was of age-old oak, polished by the industry of Mrs. Sutherland to a surface that was as slippery as ice. Crouching, Peter suddenly felt his right foot slide from under him. He fell backwards, and in a desperate effort to recover his balance pulled Michael Dene with him.

They heard the man with the torch utter an angry oath, the ray moved sharply, and they were bathed in a circle of dazzling light.

The Secret Service man scrambled to his feet, jerking his automatic from his pocket as he did so, but the mischief had been done. The man by the door raised his hand, something glittered as it fell through the ray of the torch, there was a tinkling crash of breaking glass, and a loud pop like the withdrawal of a cork from a giant champagne bottle. Before Michael Dene could raise the weapon he held in his hand he was gasping and choking as the acrid fumes of a pungent gas gripped his throat.

He heard Colgate-Jones give a grunt and break into a fit of coughing, and the man with the torch utter a muffled chuckle. And then sight and sound faded away as he slithered in an unconscious heap to the floor . . .

★   ★   ★

The first thing Michael Dene saw as he opened his eyes painfully was the huddled figure of Colgate-Jones lying in a pool of yellow sunlight. The vicar's round, usually florid face was deathly white.

For some seconds Dene stared about him in a dazed stupor, conscious only of a throbbing pain in his head and the soreness of his throat, and then, as the mist cleared slowly from his numbed brain, he remembered.

He supported the stout clergyman on his arm for a few moments and then, when he had sufficiently recovered, assisted him to his feet and then out into the garden.

'What was that infernal stuff they used?' asked the vicar. 'My throat's like a rasp.'

'Some form of gas,' answered Dene. 'They certainly won that round.'

'Did they get the key?' demanded Colgate-Jones.

Dene shook his head,

'I don't know yet,' he replied. 'Let's see if we can bring Clayton round, and then we'll have a look.'

It took them some time to restore Peter to consciousness, but they succeeded eventually, and after they had swilled their heads in cold water at the kitchen sink they felt almost normal.

The appearance of the study showed that the night intruders had made a thorough search of the place. The drawers of the writing table were open and their contents strewn about the floor. They had not been forced, but unlocked, and near a leg of the table Dene discovered a bunch of keys.

'Are these yours?' he asked Colgate-Jones.

He nodded.

'Yes,' he answered. 'They were on the small table by my bedside.'

'Which shows that they went upstairs!' said Michael Dene grimly. 'And if they went into your room they went into your room they went into the others!'

'By Jove!' exclaimed the vicar; and his face became anxious as a thought struck him. 'I wonder if anything has happened to my housekeeper and Mary?'

'You'd better go and see,' said Dene. 'There's not much doubt that they got what they came for, but I'll make sure.'

He hurried upstairs to his room, accompanied by Colgate-Jones and Peter. The stout clergyman left them at the door of the apartment to find out if the women were all right, and Dene and Peter entered the room.

Before going to bed the Secret Service man had put the Priory Key and the strip of paper on the mantelpiece, together with his watch and money. The watch and money were still there, but the strip of paper and the key had gone.

'It was so conspicuous they couldn't very well overlook it,' said Dene when he had made his discovery, and congratulated himself that his wallet containing his identification papers was in the hip pocket of the trousers he was wearing.

'Well, it doesn't matter very much. I took a copy of the contents of the key last night, and I — '

He broke off as Colgate-Jones burst into the room.

'Dene!' he said breathlessly, 'A terrible thing has happened! Mary — '

'What's happened to Miss Jordan?' broke in Peter curtly as he paused to get his breath.

'She's gone!' panted the vicar. 'Her room's all upside down and reeks of chloroform. She's gone! Those devils have taken her away!'

9

The Bald-Headed Man

Mary Jordan experienced a peculiar sensation of motion and, through the enveloping blanket of unconsciousness that shrouded her senses, was dimly aware of a gentle vibration. Over and above this was an uncomfortable feeling of sickness, and a dull throbbing ache that beat remorselessly at her brain.

She was dreaming, of course, but it was a most unpleasant dream, and she longed to be able to wake up. The sense of movement and the accompanying vibration only came to her at intervals; at others she seemed to sink into a sea of blackness, which blotted out everything.

She moaned faintly, praying that she could wake from this horrible nightmare, and then suddenly she found that she was awake, that it was no part of a bad dream, but real! The vibration was the rhythmic pulsing of an engine.

She looked around her with dazed eyes, and saw that she was in a car, accompanied by two men, who were engaged in binding her wrists and ankles; men whose faces were hidden behind masks of black.

Terror gripped her and she gave a little cry.

'Here, stop that!' snarled one of the men. 'If you don't want to be hurt, keep quiet!'

She stared up at him fearfully. What had happened? How had she managed to get into the clutches of these unknown and terrifying people?

'What — what are you doing with me?' she asked huskily.

'You'll be all right,' grunted the man who had spoken. 'That is, if you're sensible. Lie still and don't ask questions.'

His companion finished knotting the rope at her ankles and sat back on the seat.

Glancing through the windows of the swiftly moving car she saw that it was daylight. From her position she could see very little else. The car seemed to be travelling at a high speed, but whether they were passing through towns or country she was unaware.

The terror that her curiosity had overcome returned, intensified. Were they taking her somewhere to suffer the same fate as Norris?

In the sudden panic that overwhelmed her at the thought she tried to struggle up, but with a muttered oath the man nearest her forced her back on the cushions.

'Keep quiet, will you?' he growled. 'I warned you before.'

Her eyes, wide with terror, stared up into the masked face.

'We're nearly there now,' a voice exclaimed.

'Good thing, too,' was the answer. 'I shan't be sorry to get a bite of food and some sleep. Who were those fellows at the parson's?'

'Friends of his, I suppose,' said the second man. 'Lucky you brought the bomb with you. It gave me a shock when I saw the three of them crouching in the corner. I bet they're not feeling too good now!' The speaker chuckled. 'What do you make of that verse?'

'I don't make anything of it,' was the reply. 'It sounds a lot of nonsense to me.'

'The Guv'nor'll find out what it means,' declared the other confidently. 'He was pretty quick over the other.'

They lapsed into silence, and Mary puzzled her brains to find a meaning for this scrappy conversation she had over-heard. What was this verse they were talking about, and what was the reference to a bomb?

The car swung to the right, continued in this new direction for half a mile or so, and then slowing, came to a halt.

'Here we are,' grunted the man who had spoken last; and opening the door he got out.

A third man, whom she had not seen before but who, she concluded, had been driving the car, joined him. He was dressed in a neat chauffeur's uniform, and the upper half of his face was hidden behind goggles. The glass partition dividing the interior of the car from the driving seat was covered with a blind, so she had been unable to see who had been in charge of the machine.

The man in the chauffeur's uniform

took a key from his pocket and unlocked the door. She was carried into a narrow hall, furnished sparsely with a few articles of decrepit furniture. They took her through to a room at the back, obviously the kitchen, and laid her down on the stone-flagged floor.

'If you try to make a fuss you'll get hurt!' said the man who had warned her before. 'For your own sake I advise you to keep quiet!'

He turned abruptly and went out, followed by his two companions. The heavy door slammed to, and she heard the rasp of bolts as they were shot into their sockets.

Mary lay for a moment or two after they had gone, with closed eyes, fighting the terror which threatened to get the upper hand, and then, when she had more or less succeeded in stifling her fear, she opened her eyes and took stock of her surroundings.

Her head still ached dully, and her throat was dry and parched. She would have given almost anything for a warm drink.

From somewhere beyond the locked

door she could hear the faint sound of voices, and wondered whether her captors were discussing what was to happen to her.

Again she tried to puzzle out the reason why she had been brought to this place, and failed to achieve any satisfactory explanation. The man who had killed her brother was in the hands of the police, so it was ridiculous to suppose that he had had anything to do with it. And yet, in some way, her present position must be linked with Norris's death. There was nothing else to account for it.

She was still trying to find a reasonable explanation when she heard soft footsteps approaching. They stopped at the door and there came to her ears the rasp of the bolts as they were drawn back. Slowly the door swung inwards, and a man came softly into the room. She had expected to see one of the three men who had been with the car, but the newcomer was a stranger.

He was of medium height, and rather fat, and was dressed in an immaculate suit of some grey material. The collar that encircled his neck was snowy white and below the neat knot of his light grey tie glittered a diamond pin. But it was his face that held Mary's eyes and sent a cold shiver down her spine. It was round and chubby; not the florid chubbiness that marked the jovial features of Colgate-Jones but an unhealthy, lard-coloured flabbiness from which the small, pale-blue eyes stared steadily. A thin gash of crimson marked the tiny mouth, and, to add to the repulsiveness of his appearance, he was utterly and completely bald.

There was something about him that reminded her of a snake. Possibly it was the peculiar shape of his hairless head, for it was flat, with the result that his forehead looked unusually low.

For some seconds he stood in silence, regarding her with those cold, emotionless eyes.

'So,' he remarked at last, and his voice held a faint lisping quality, which in some peculiar way, added to his general unpleasantness, 'So you are the sister of Norris Jordan, eh? Your brother gave us a lot of trouble. A lot of trouble! I hope you are going to be more sensible.'

She passed the tip of her tongue over her dry lips.

'I don't know what you mean,' she said. 'Why have I been brought here?'

'You have been brought here,' said the bald man, 'because we wish you to answer a few questions. We are anxious to discover the names and addresses of your brother's intimate friends.'

The question sounded familiar, and it flashed through her mind that it had been put to her in a different form by the lean-faced, grey-eyed man who had been with Colgate-Jones on her arrival.

'I know none of my brother's intimate friends,' she answered.

He pursed his lips so that his mouth looked like a crimson spot in the grey-white expanse of his face.

'I should advise you to think carefully, Miss Jordan,' he remarked smoothly. 'I assure you that I am not to be trifled with. I have gone to a lot of trouble to bring you here, and I do not intend that that trouble shall be wasted. You will please reconsider your answer.'

'What is the use,' she said. 'I have told you the truth. I know none of my brother's intimate friends, with the exception of Mr. Colgate-Jones. What is the reason for this questioning?'

'That is entirely my affair,' he replied. 'I should remind you that if you prove stubborn there are ways and means of making you speak. They are both unpleasant, and painful, and I should be reluctant to have to use them, but I shall do so without hesitation if you force me to it.' The mincing voice was calm, the words quietly spoken, but they sent a shiver through Mary Jordan, and she felt the blood recede from her face.

'If you killed me I could not tell you what I don't know,' she said.

'Perhaps you would prefer being killed to what I have in mind!' he said. 'However, I will give you an hour to think it over. Take my advice and be sensible.'

He turned on his heel and went out, closing and bolting the door behind him, leaving Mary alone to face as best she could the unknown terrors that lay in store for her.

10

The Second Clue

Peter stared at Colgate-Jones, his face pale. 'Are you sure . . . ?' he began, and the vicar interrupted him.

'There's no possible doubt!' he said. 'They've got Mary! What are we going to do about it?'

'Take me to the room she occupied.' said Michael Dene curtly and the stout gentleman obeyed.

At the door of the large, pleasantly-furnished apartment Dene paused and allowed his eyes to travel swiftly round the room.

Peter and Colgate-Jones waited anxiously while the Secret Service man completed his search, and the former's face fell when Dene reported his negative result.

'We've got to do something! Think of it, man — that girl in the hands of those fiends — '

'I am thinking about it!' snapped Dene

irritably. 'And if you can suggest anything I shall be glad to hear it. At the moment I'm forced to admit I can't.'

'D'you mean we've just got to sit down quietly and do nothing?' demanded Peter. 'They may serve her the same way as they did her brother!'

Michael Dene shook his head.

'I don't think they're likely to do that,' he said, his brows knitted together in a frown. 'It's fairly obvious why they've taken her. They're hoping that she will be able to supply them with the names of the people to whom Jordan sent the result of his discoveries. Which proves that they must have overheard what he told you at the cottage before he was killed.' He turned to Colgate-Jones. 'Before we go any further I think we ought to see whether your housekeeper's all right.'

The clergyman uttered an exclamation.

'By Jove, I forgot all about her!' he cried. 'The shock of finding Mary gone put it clean out of my mind. She sleeps on the floor above.'

He hurried up the stairs, with Michael Dene and Peter at his heels, stopping before a closed door on the landing. Without ceremony he grasped the handle and flung it open.

Mrs. Sutherland lay on a disordered bed, her wrists and ankles bound with strips torn from one of the sheets, a handkerchief tightly fastened about her mouth. Her indignant eyes stared at them as they crowded in the open doorway.

'Get a knife from the kitchen,' said Dene to Peter, and while he was gone went over and untied the gag.

He had to administer water before the woman could speak, and her story added very little to the information already in their possession.

'Now,' said Michael Dene, after filling and lighting his pipe, 'our most sensible course at the moment is to find the solution to Jordan's second clue. On the strip of paper we found in the Prior's Key there's a mention of Paul and Wu L — something or other. The latter is obviously part of the name of a Chinaman. If we can find slip number two we shall probably discover the surname of the person called Paul and the rest of the other name.

This may give us something to work on.'

'All I'm anxious to do,' muttered Peter, 'is to find that poor girl before any harm can come to her.'

'So am I,' said Dene, 'and I think by discovering the meaning of that rhyme we may go a long way to doing so.' Colgate-Jones agreed, and Dene spread out on his knee the copy he had made of Jordan's strip.

'Let's take it line by line,' he said, 'and see what we can make of it. 'A key suggests to the mind a lock, and it's not hard to find'. Now that, obviously, does not refer to the type of lock in which you insert a key at all, because the whole object of the rhyme is to give us a line to the person who holds the second slip. It contains not only a clue to the identity of the person but also that person's whereabouts, and if you think for a moment no ordinary lock could do this, so therefore it must mean — '

'A water-lock!' broke in Colgate-Jones, and the Secret Service man nodded.

'Exactly!' he said. 'A water-lock!'

The clergyman pursed his lips

'That doesn't help us very much,' he said gloomily. 'There are forty-seven locks on the river.'

'And numerous canals with a few hundred more,' grunted Peter.

'Exactly!' said Michael Dene again. 'Therefore the second part of the rhyme must narrow the locality down to one particular lock. 'A child will help, so seek one out'. How does that help us?'

'It doesn't help me at all,' said Peter candidly.

Colgate-Jones said nothing, but his forehead wrinkled into a frown of concentration.

''A child will help, so seek one out',' he murmured under his breath.

'We'll come to that later,' said Dene. 'The last line, 'And keep, ergo, free from doubt' is easy, and confirms the fact that it is a water-lock we're looking for.'

'Why? What does it mean?' demanded Peter.

The Secret Service man smiled.

'Well,' he explained, 'there was no reason why Jordan should have used the

Latin word 'ergo' unless he had a very good object to serve. The English equivalent 'therefore' fits more easily. He used 'ergo' because no other word would do.'

'I don't follow,' grunted Peter.

'And keep, ergo, free from doubt,' repeated Dene. 'It you cut off the last two letters of 'ergo' and add what remains to 'keep' you've got the word 'keeper'. So the man we want to find is the keeper of some specified lock or other.'

'Let's look up the list of locks on the Thames,' suggested Colgate-Jones, 'and see if that will help.'

He got up and rummaged among his bookshelves, returning with a small, red-covered volume which he opened and hastily turned the pages.

'Here you are. Richmond, Teddington — '

Peter uttered an exclamation.

'Can that be it?' he said eagerly. 'Ted could be the name of a child.'

Michael Dene screwed up his face dubiously.

'Maybe,' he said. 'But it doesn't seem

definite enough to me. Go on, Jones.'

'Molesey, Sunbury, Shepperton, Chertsey, Penton Hook,' continued the vicar, running a fat finger up the list. 'Bell Weir, Old Windsor, Romney, Boveney, Bray, Boulters, Cookham, Marlow, Temple, Hurley, Hambledon, Marsh, Shiplake, Sonning.' He paused. 'Sonning might be it,' he said, looking. 'Son, that would be a child.'

'It's too vague,' muttered Dene, frowning, and then suddenly his face cleared and he slapped his knee. 'What fools we are!' he exclaimed. 'Of course, it's obvious. Temple Lock!'

Peter stared at him.

'Where does the child come in?' he asked, and Dene smiled.

'Surely you've heard of Shirley Temple?' he remarked.

'Of course!' cried Colgate-Jones. 'You've got it, Dene! The man who holds the second section of poor Jordan's secret is the keeper of Temple Lock. I don't think there's any doubt of it.'

Michael Dene rose to his feet and knocked the ashes out of his pipe.

'Is there anywhere round here where

we can hire a fast launch?'

The vicar nodded. 'You can get one at the boathouse,' he said, 'a few yards down the river from here.'

'Then I'll hire one at once,' said the Secret Service man, 'and run up to Temple Lock.'

'If you'll wait a second,' said Colgate-Jones, 'I'll go and change. This is hardly the type of job to tackle in a clerical collar.'

'Are you coming with us?' asked Dene in surprise.

'I most certainly am!' said the vicar decisively. 'Nothing short of an earthquake would keep me out. Jordan was a friend of mine and his sister was in my charge when those brutes kidnapped her. I feel a moral responsibility to see the thing through.'

'But what about your parish duties — ' began Dene, and the vicar cut him short.

'My holidays started this morning,' he said, his round, red face one huge grin, 'so you needn't worry about that. I'm going to see this thing through, I tell you.'

'I'll be glad to have you with me,' said

Dene. 'But I must warn you that it's a dangerous business.'

'Damn the danger!' said the Reverend Colgate-Jones cheerfully, and hurried away to change.

11

The Name of Michael Dene

Never had the time seemed to pass so slowly to Mary Jordan as the hour during which she awaited the return of the bald-headed man. She was terribly frightened — the more so because what lay ahead of her was unknown — but she refused to give way to her fear. A certain pride made her resolve that whatever happened she would not give the unpleasant-faced man the satisfaction of knowing that she was afraid of him. That she had good cause to be she never doubted. There was something in those hard, cold, light eyes that warned her she could expect no mercy if she interfered with his plans.

A stumbling step broke in on her thoughts. The hour then, which the bald-headed man had given her, was up. She heard the rasping of the bolts, and braced herself to meet whatever ordeal lay in store.

The door opened and one of the men who travelled in the car with her entered. She had expected to see the fat man, and experienced something of a shock at the advent of the other. He crossed to her side quickly, and as she saw the knife he held in his hand her flesh crept. But there was no basis for the fear that the sight of the keen blade had created. Stooping, without a word, he severed the cords at her ankles.

'Get up!' he ordered curtly. But although she tried to obey she found it impossible. The restricting cords had stopped her circulation and numbed her limbs, and he had to pull her roughly to her feet and support her.

'Where are we going?' she asked.

'Not very far,' he replied. 'The Guv'nor wants to see, you, and if you're wise you'll do what he asks.'

He led her along a dark passage, paused before a half closed door, and pushed it open without removing his hand from her arm. She was thrust into a square room, larger than the kitchen, with a low ceiling, and furnished shabbily but comfortably. A coal fire burned in the grate, and the air was stale and fetid as though the windows were seldom open. The bald-headed man was sitting in a chair by the fire, smoking a cigar.

'I hope you have thought over what I said a little while ago,' he said, 'and that you are prepared to comply with my request.'

'I told you then, and I can only repeat it now,' she answered, 'that what you ask is impossible because I don't know.'

He looked at her, and it required all her strength to meet those eyes without flinching.

'I was hoping,' he murmured, 'that you were not going to persist in your denial. I assure you, Miss Jordan, that it will only have the effect of making things very unpleasant for you. For I intend to have that information at any cost — at any cost! You understand me?'

She understood him only too well, and the knowledge terrified her, but she wasn't going to show it if she could help it.

'I cannot give you information which I do not know myself,' she answered, striving with all her force to keep her voice steady. 'My brother spent most of his time away, and I only saw him at rare intervals.'

There was a moment's silence.

'Who were the two men,' he went on, 'who were staying with Mr. Jones?'

She shook her head.

'They were strangers to me,' she replied. 'I had never seen either of them before. They were introduced to me as Mr. Pinner and Mr. Dene — '

'Say that again!' he snapped harshly, springing to his feet, and when she complied; 'What was this man like? Tell me, girl — quickly!'

'He was tall and rather lean,' she answered huskily, 'with grey eyes — '

'It's the same man!' he muttered. 'Why didn't those fools tell me?'

Suddenly he stopped by the door, jerked it open, and called harshly:

'Muller! Muller! Come here at once!'

There was a short delay, and then the man who had brought her from the kitchen came in quickly.

'What is it?' he asked. 'Has — '

'Take the girl away!' broke in the bald man curtly. 'Take her away and tie her up securely! I've no more time to deal with her at the moment. Take her away and then come back here!'

'Why? What has happened?' began the man, startled by the agitation in the other's tone.

'The worst that could have happened,' was the reply. 'Do you know who that man was at the vicarage? The man you and Casler gassed? Michael Dene, the cleverest man in the British Secret Service! The head of the Special Branch! Listen to me. I have a plan, and we must move fast!'

12

At the Lock

Old Tom Holding, the weather-beaten keeper of Temple Lock, leaned against one of his iron sluice wheels and gazed meditatively downstream at the slowly moving river. On this bright morning there were few pleasure boats about; a girl was rowing leisurely across to the opposite bank, and further down, near the bend, a four-oared skiff was out for sculling practice, the lightly-clad figures of the young men it contained bending back and forth to the rhythmic stroke of their oars.

The lock-keeper took his pipe from between his lips and spat thoughtfully.

The newspaper which he had read on the previous night had given him something of a shock, for in it he had seen the account of Norris Jordan's death. Well, he had been the type of man who wasn't born to die in his bed. He recollected the many yarns they had had together. A nice fellow, nothing stuck-up about him. Many were the times he had come sauntering along the towpath, and, after a cheery greeting, sat for hours watching the craft pass through the lock. Sometimes he'd scarcely speak, at others he'd rattle on till you couldn't get a word in edgeways. A moody chap, but interesting when he liked to talk. And now he wouldn't talk any more.

Away in the distance he saw a motor launch coming rapidly upstream, the white diverging lines of its wash glittering in the sunlight. He watched it idly, his thoughts still centred on the tragic death of his friend. Jordan 'ud never come now to claim the little object he had sent from Germany. Funny thing it were too, the brass figure of a dancing child. Nice bit of work, and probably valuable, though why Mr. J. had sent it to him he couldn't make out. It wasn't a present, for in his letter he had asked him to keep it carefully until he came for it himself or sent someone with his authority. Well, he'd stuck it on his mantelpiece and there it was, but it was a funny thing to have done all the same.

He waited, watching the little boat as it drew nearer. Trim little craft. His keen eyes made out the name on the bows — 'River Girl'. He couldn't recollect her. She'd never been through his lock before, and it didn't look as if she was coming through now. She was making for the towpath shore a few yards away.

He eyed the boat as it drew slowly in, watched it come to a stop, and saw the lean-faced man who had been driving get out and tie up to a ring in the bank. His companions followed him, and they all three began to walk towards the lock.

Michael Dene caught sight of the thick-set figure in the peaked cap and turned to Colgate-Jones.

'That's our man, I think,' he said.

They breasted the slope and came into the trim garden, gay with flowers.

'Good morning!' greeted Dene, as he drew level with the man who was lounging against the iron wheel. 'Are you the lock-keeper?'

Tom Holding took the pipe from

between his lips and nodded.

'That's me, sir,' he said.

'I'd like a word with you,' continued the Secret Service man. 'I believe you knew Mr. Norris Jordan?'

The lock-keeper eyed him steadily before replying.

'Ay, I did, sir,' he answered at length,

'I don't know whether you are aware,' Dene went on, 'that Jordan was murdered a few nights ago at a cottage in Berkshire.'

'I read about it,' said Tom Holding. 'A feller named Clayton did him in.'

'I am engaged in investigating the crime,' said Dene, without confirming this last statement, 'and I understand that some time before he died Jordan sent you a certain object with instructions to keep it until he came to collect it. Isn't that right?'

'That's right, sir,' said the lock-keeper, and his face was a little puzzled. 'He sent me the figure of a dancing child. A pretty little thing it is, an' he asked me to keep it until he called for it or sent someone with his authority to collect it.'

Michael Dene's eyes gleamed. The

double meaning contained in the line, 'A child will help, so seek one out,' was now apparent.

'I should be much obliged if you would let me have it,' he said.

Tom Holding knocked the ashes from his pipe and stowed it away in his trouser pocket.

'Come over to the lock-house, sir,' he said, 'an' I'll give it to you. It's a funny thing,' he went on as they followed him into the building, 'but I was wonderin' this mornin' whether I ought to inform the police about that little image. What's it got to do with Mr. Jordan's death, sir?'

'It may have nothing to do with it,' answered Dene, for he had no wish to take the lock-keeper into his confidence. 'You will realize, however, that it is the duty of the police to follow up any possible clue, and since an examination of Mr. Jordan's papers showed that he had sent this thing to you for safe keeping, we thought we'd better come and collect it.'

Opening the door he led the way into a tiny sitting room, scrupulously clean and comfortable in a Spartan way. Crossing to the narrow mantelpiece he took down a little brass statue about six inches high, representing a child in ballet skirts, pirouetting on tiptoe.

'That's it, sir,' he said, and handed it to Dene.

The Secret Service Man took it and examined it carefully. It appeared quite solid, and its weight seemed to bear out this supposition. At the same time appearances in this case were obviously deceptive, for he knew that in some manner it contained another section of the documents on which Jordan had written down his discoveries.

The sharp staccato blast of a siren came from outside, and the lock-keeper, who had been staring at Dene, roused himself.

'Excuse me, sir,' he said, 'but that's the Reading boat waitin' to come through. I'll have to go and open the lock.'

He left them, hurrying away to attend to his duties, and Dene continued his examination of the little object in his hand. It was not as easy to solve the secret of this image as it had been with the Prior's

Key. He concluded that the interior must be hollow, but there appeared no means of reaching it, short of breaking the thing up.

He mentioned this fact to his companions.

'We'd better take it and examine it at our leisure,' he said. 'I'll leave a receipt for the lock-keeper.'

He took a scrap of paper and his fountain pen from his pocket, hastily wrote a receipt, and signed it with the name that had appeared on the warrant card.

'Perhaps it's just as well not to open it here — even if we knew how.'

They came out of the lock-house and walked towards the edge of the lock. A big passenger steamer was moving slowly in through the upper gate. Michael Dene watched interestedly as it was brought to rest in the lock and the gates closed behind it. A swarthy-faced, thickset man was standing near them, also apparently interested in the boat.

The lock-keeper came hurrying towards the lower gate and began to turn the wheel, which opened the sluices. They heard the roar of the water as it poured out of the lock and watched the steamer slowly falling.

'We'd better wait and thank the keeper before we go,' began Dene, 'and then — '

He never completed the sentence. Something struck him sharply in the middle of the back, and with an exclamation he staggered forward.

He had been standing within a foot of the edge of the lock. For a moment he swayed desperately, trying to recover his balance, then fell with a splash into the turgid water.

It closed over his head as he sank like a stone and mechanically he struck out, but giant hands seemed to be pulling his legs, and strive as he might he could not reach the surface.

With a thrill of horror he realised why. He was in the grip of the suction of the sluices! Hundreds of tons of water were pouring through those submerged openings, and the enormous pressure was taking him with it. The finest swimmer in the world could not overcome that tremendous force.

His brain worked quickly. There was one chance, and one chance only, and that was of the slenderest.

He dived, praying that he would reach the open sluices and not be crushed against the solid gate.

The water roared in his ears with the noise of thunder. Dimly, somewhere below him, he could see a faint, greenish-yellow light. Down, down he went, twisting and turning like a cork in that rushing maelstrom. The roar grew louder and the pent-up air in his lungs made him feel as though his chest was bursting,

He was sucked along quickly in the grip of that relentless torrent, a helpless atom, and then his head struck something with stunning force!

He felt a momentary agonising pain envelop his whole body, and then the noise faded to silence and blackness blotted out everything!

13

The Man at the Window

Gradually, very gradually, the darkness began to disperse. It was like the slow drawing back of a curtain over the window of a darkened room. Vaguely, through a mist that floated before his eyes, Michael Dene saw dim, unrecognizable faces flitting about him, and felt an inexplicable rhythmic movement of his arms that puzzled him.

The fog that obscured his brain was rapidly clearing. He saw that the face that had been peering at him belonged to a stranger, a small man with a bald head, who was kneeling on the grass beside him. Beyond he caught a glimpse of the anxious faces of Peter Clayton and Colgate-Jones; beyond them again a little knot of people.

'Feeling better now?'

It was the voice of the bald-headed man with the moustache who spoke, and with an effort Dene replied.

'Yes.' The words were husky and scarcely audible. 'My head hurts a bit,'

'I don't wonder,' was the reply. 'You've got a nasty wound, but you can think yourself lucky you're not dead!'

Michael Dene struggled up on one elbow. He was lying on the towpath, and around him was gathered a little crowd of curious sightseers. The strange murmuring noise was still going on, and he was able to place it now. It was the distant roar of the weir.

'By Jove, you gave us a turn!' said Colgate-Jones slipping an arm around his shoulders. 'I thought it was all over when you failed to come up. You must have gone through the sluices. Luckily Clayton saw you bob up the other side of the lock gate, but you were unconscious when we pulled you out. I went for a doctor and he administered artificial respiration.'

It was the nearest thing Dene wanted to experience, and he said so.

'Help me up,' he muttered, 'and let's get away from this crowd.'

With the assistance of Peter, Colgate-Jones managed to get him on his feet. His knees were wobbly and the movement made his head swim, but after a moment or two he was able to summon up sufficient strength to walk unsteadily between them the short distance to the lock-keeper's little house. 'You'd better get those wet things off,' said the doctor, who had accompanied them. 'I don't think I can do any more for the moment. A stiff brandy and soda and you ought to be all right.'

Colgate-Jones paid his fee, and when he had gone turned to Dene, who was huddled in Tom Holding's only armchair.

'How did you manage to fall in?' he inquired.

'It wasn't an accident!' answered the Secret Service man. 'It was attempted murder!'

Peter uttered an exclamation.

'Murder!' he echoed.

Dene nodded weakly.

'Yes,' he answered. 'That swarthy faced man who was standing near me. Didn't you see him?'

Colgate-Jones shook his head.

'I saw nothing until I heard the splash,' he replied. 'I was looking at the boat.'

'Everybody thinks it was an accident,' said Peter.

'Let them continue to think so,' answered Michael Dene. 'We don't want a lot of unnecessary publicity.'

A consultation with the lock-keeper extracted the information that there was a hotel a short distance away from the lock, and by the time they reached it Dene's clothes were almost dry. He explained to the sympathetic landlord that he had accidentally fallen into the river, and a brandy and soda and a hot bath removed the last traces of his adventure. When they had finished lunch he was feeling fit for anything.

The little inn was practically deserted, and in the seclusion of the bar-parlour, which the landlord placed at their disposal, they discussed their next move.

'We must watch our step,' said Dene as he examined the little statuette, which they had secured from Tom Holding. 'In some way or other these people we are up against are aware of my identity. There can be no other explanation for that attempt at the lock, and I have no doubt that they are watching us every minute.'

'And they have the advantage of us,' remarked Peter, 'because they know us and we don't know them.'

'Quite,' agreed Dene. 'That's just it. I am hoping, however, that the second section of poor Jordan's evidence will level that up a little.'

'How do you mean?' inquired Colgate-Jones.

'You remember on the first strip,' explained the Secret Service man, 'there was the Christian name of Paul and a mention of Wu L — something or other. I am hoping that the rest of it will be on this second strip, though I'm hanged if I can find any means of reaching the interior of this figure.'

He had been twisting and turning the brass statue of the dancing-girl about in his fingers while speaking.

'There must be some means of opening it,' grunted Colgate-Jones. 'But we can't wait. Go and get some pliers, Mr. Clayton.'

Peter went out and presently returned with some strong pliers and a spanner.

He unscrewed the jaws of the spanner,

slipped the waist of the tiny figure between them, and tightened them up. With all his strength Dene twisted. There was a snap, and Colgate-Jones bent eagerly forward.

'The thing is hollow!' he breathed.

The Secret Service man nodded.

'Yes,' he said, and pointed to the fracture, 'and the waist was originally made to unscrew. You can see the thread.'

He turned the little figure upside down and shook it. A thin roll of paper fell out on to the table as he did so. Under the interested eyes of the other two, Dene rapidly unrolled it.

The paper was a facsimile of the strip they had found concealed in the Prior's Key, and as he spread it out on the table Peter and Colgate-Jones bent over his shoulder and read the wording.

2.
ase of
result
There
will
ople be . . .
whose ob . . .

have acq . . .
on which . . .
intention
thus
the
nt of wa . . .
fteen y . . .
reserve
lace so . . .
not be . . .
when th . . .
me forw . . .
ames of
Lenoir, A
i Fu a . . .
rganiser
final m . . .
27th at
ghamshire.
nce bef . . .
plot, bu..
able to

Two names near the end caught Dene's eyes and he drew in his breath sharply.

'Lenoir!' he breathed. 'Paul Lenoir and Wu Li Fu! Good heavens, they can't be mixed up in this!'

'Who are they, anyway?' asked Peter.

'Paul Lenoir is a multi-millionaire,' answered Dene, his brows drawn together. 'The French armament king, and Wu Li Fu is one of the richest mandarins in China!'

He took his wallet from his pocket, and from it removed the damp copy of the strip they had found in the Prior's Key. Carefully he placed it alongside the second strip. It joined up fairly accurately and they read the result:

1. 2.
In case of
the result
years. There
which will
The people be . . .
men whose ob . . .
They have acq . . .
invention which . . .
their intention
reserve, thus
it at the
the event of wa . . .
For fifteen y . . .

gold reserve
a place so . . .
have not be . . .
and when th . . .
to come forw . . .
The names of
Paul Lenoir, A
Wu Li Fu a . . .
the organiser
The final m . . .
July 27th at
Buckinghamshire,
evidence bef . . .
this plot, bu . . .
being able to

'It doesn't help us very much, so far as the plot is concerned,' said Michael Dene. 'It appears to be something to do with an invention, and obviously Lenoir and Li Fu are two of the group concerned in the conspiracy.'

He turned over the second strip and pointed to the rhyme on the back.

'Here's our third clue,' he said. 'Let's see what we can make of it.'

'Music, without player or score,
Will lead to where a man of law
Reads Shakespeare by a shady brook,
And will, if asked, give back the book.'

Colgate-Jones repeated the line below his breath.

'The last part of it is obvious,' he said. 'Jordan's third section is concealed in some book or other — probably a copy of Shakespeare. But what does the first part of it mean?'

Michael Dene shook his head slowly.

'I don't know — ' he began, and swung round as a shadow darkened the light from the open window.

He caught a momentary glimpse of a face peering in at them, and then the little casement was empty. But that one glimpse had been enough for him to recognise the eavesdropper. It was the swarthy-faced man of the lock!

14

Murder!

Dene was out of his chair and had reached the little garden at the back of the inn which the bar-parlour overlooked before Peter and Colgate-Jones realised what had happened. But there was no sign of the dark-featured eavesdropper. A path led to the road, and hurrying along this the Secret Service man looked to right and left. A car was just disappearing round the bend, but there was nothing else in sight, and he concluded that it was by this means that the listener had made his escape.

As he turned disappointedly away to re-enter the inn, the others joined him.

'What was the matter?' demanded Peter anxiously. 'What did you see?'

The Secret Service man explained briefly.

'You didn't see him?' he concluded.

They both shook their heads.

'I only just caught a glimpse of him,' went on Dene. 'If he hadn't made the mistake of momentarily obscuring the light I shouldn't have known he was there either.'

'Are you sure it was the same fellow?' muttered Colgate-Jones.

'Positive!' declared Michael Dene. 'That was the man who pushed me into the lock, without any doubt whatever.'

'He had some nerve to come snooping back here!' growled Peter. 'I should have thought he'd have made himself scarce after his murder plan failed.'

'The question is,' continued Dene when they were once more in the cool little sitting room, 'how much did the fellow overhear?'

'That,' said Colgate-Jones, 'depends on how long he was there.'

'I'm afraid he was there long enough,' said the Secret Service man, 'to hear us discussing the rhyme. You read it aloud, if you remember.'

The clergyman nodded, frowning.

'I'd no idea there was anyone about,' he said.

'Of course you didn't,' said Dene. 'Neither did any of us, though we might have guessed it if we had any sense. We ought to have known that after following us from the vicarage they wouldn't have abandoned their surveillance. I've no doubt that our olive-skinned friend is now hurrying as hard as he can to inform his employer of the clue that leads to Jordan's third section.'

'Well, they'll be clever if they can make anything of it,' growled Peter, picking up the strip of paper and staring at it gloomily. 'Look here, Dene, what are we going to do about Miss Jordan? We seem to have more or less forgotten her.'

'I haven't forgotten her by any means!' retorted Michael Dene. 'But as I said before Clayton, our only chance of rescuing her is to discover the people at the bottom of this company, which Jordan has unearthed. To do that we've got to find the other five sections, or the majority of them.'

'That may take us weeks!' grumbled Peter.

'We can't afford to let it take us weeks!'

said Dene. 'Apart from Miss Jordan's danger, this thing comes to a head on the twenty-seventh of July, and it's now the twenty-eighth of June. We've got just under a month to round up these people and put a stop to the plot, whatever it is; and I don't mind telling you it's not a day too long. If we can find the whole of Jordan's report it's going to help enormously. But even when we've found that, don't forget we've got to prove his allegations.

'These men are playing for big stakes,' the Secret Service man went on. 'Jordan told you that their principal object was money, and if that's the case it must be a colossal sum, for Paul Lenoir is already a millionaire several times over and the extent of Li Fu's wealth is incalculable. If the rest of the group are in the same category, then money is no object with them. To attain their ends they'll spend it like water, and that makes them very powerful.'

'When you put it like that,' said Peter, a little huskily, 'it seems as if we were facing an impossible task.'

'By no means!' said Dene quickly. 'They may be powerful — they are powerful — but don't forget we've got the whole of the British Secret Service behind us, plus the entire organization of Scotland Yard. Although we can't make bricks without straw, once we've got a shred of proof those two organisations will move, and they'll move with the certainty and precision of a steam hammer, and crush this conspiracy out of existence along with the people responsible for it.'

He pulled his pipe from his pocket and borrowed Colgate-Jones' pouch, his own tobacco having been rendered un-smokable by his immersion in the lock.

'Our principal object,' he continued, stuffing tobacco into the bowl, 'is to discover the plot these people have hatched and put an end to it. Therefore, although I am fully alive to the danger in which Mary Jordan resides at present, and am willing to use my utmost endeavours to rescue her from it, we must regard her position as of secondary importance.'

Peter uttered an angry exclamation.

'I know what you are going to say,' said

Dene quickly, 'but if you think for a moment you'll see that I am right. According to what Jordan told you, this conspiracy means the ruin of Great Britain and the over-throw of civilisation, and to prevent that we must be prepared, if necessary — I hope it won't be — to sacrifice everything to stop it.'

There was silence as he struck a match and lit his pipe.

'You're quite right, Dene,' said Colgate-Jones soberly. 'Quite right! But the thought of Mary in the hands of those thieves makes me see red.'

'It doesn't exactly cheer me,' admitted the Secret Service man, 'and I don't think you need worry too much. I've got an idea that no harm will come to her at the moment, and before it does we may have her safely back again.'

He walked over to the table and picked up the two slips of paper.

'Now,' he said, 'I think our next move is to settle up with the landlord here and get back to your place, Jones. We can do nothing more until we've solved this rhyme.'

They both agreed with him, and after

paying the landlord they made their way down to the river where the little launch was still tethered.

It was nearly five o'clock when they returned it to the launch works from which they had hired it and made their way back to the vicarage. They had kept a sharp lookout for anyone who might be trailing them, but they had seen nobody.

The Secret Service man was feeling a little irritable as he settled down next morning to tackle the third clue, but the morning passed, as had done the previous night, without bringing them any nearer to the solution of it. By lunch time they had to admit that so far it had beaten all their efforts to extract a meaning from the rhyme.

'I've thought of everything,' said Colgate-Jones gloomily, 'and I can't make head nor tail of it.'

'It's the first two lines that are important,' grunted Peter, 'but I'm dashed if I can think what he's getting at.'

'I'm afraid I'm in the same boat,' confessed Dene. 'We'll give it a rest this afternoon and try again this evening.

Perhaps if we come fresh to it we may hit on the solution.'

But it was destined that the meaning of Norris Jordan's rhyme should be offered to them without effort on their part, and it was Colgate-Jones who made the discovery.

They were having tea on the little lawn in front of the vicarage when the evening paper arrived. Peter and Dene, with knitted brows, were still wrestling with the problem that the dead journalist had left, and the clergyman, seeing their preoccupation, began rather desultorily to glance through the news. His eyes fell on a two-column spread on the front page.

MURDERED INN KEEPER
TRAGEDY IN KENTISH VILLAGE

'The Aeolian Harp, an old-fashioned inn in the village of Meopham, near Gravesend, formed the setting of a terrible tragedy which occurred during the early hours this morning.

'The landlord. Mr. Martin Judge, was discovered dead in the taproom when the potman came as usual at seven o' clock to start work. The unfortunate man had been stabbed, and there is little doubt that it was murder, and that robbery was the motive for the crime . . . '

*　*　*

So far Colgate-Jones read, and then he started up with an exclamation.

'Dene!' he cried excitedly, 'I've got it! Jordan's third clue! Listen to this!' Hurriedly he read the account of the murder. 'So you see?' he went on. 'Music without player or score will lead to where a man of law . . . ' An Aeolian harp is an instrument played by the wind — '

'And Judge was the name of the man who was killed!' breathed Peter.

Michael Dene took the paper gravely and scanned the news item.

'I think you're right,' he said, and his face set grimly. 'We've been forestalled! In this instance our unknown antagonists have been cleverer than we.' Abruptly he rose to his feet. 'Come on,' he said. 'We'll pick up my car and drive down to

Meopham at once. There's just a chance they may have left something behind at the Aeolian Harp that will put us on their trail!'

15

The Man in Control

The man who sat hunched up at the big littered desk was not much to look at, and yet in some indefinable way his shrivelled body radiated power. Whether it lay in the slate-grey eyes that were so seldom opened to their fullest extent, or whether it lay in the thin-lipped mouth with its drooping corners and the aggressive jutting chin, it was impossible to say. More likely it emanated from the brain behind the broad forehead. Certainly it did not come from anything purely physical, for the man was thin and underdeveloped, his chest narrow, and his stature below medium height. His biography was graven deeply in his face; the hard mouth was unyielding and without humour, the eyes keen and without compassion, the nostrils pinched and ungenerous.

Morgan Stenson had started life in the gutter, and by his own unaided efforts had raised himself to the position of the richest man in England. His income ran into seven figures, and only four of these were noughts. Few people could say, with accuracy, in how many pies this wizened man had a skinny finger; fewer could have estimated the total extent of his wealth, for Morgan Stenson had a poor opinion of humanity and kept most of these things to himself.

Stel Water Manor, this house in which he spent most of his time, had once been the property of Lord Overstream, and the means by which it had come into his possession does much to reveal Morgan Stenson's character.

He had been invited by Overstream, who at that time was Chairman of one of his companies, to spend a weekend at the lovely old Manor House, which had been in the Overstream family for generations. The moment he had seen it he had longed to possess it, not because of its beauty — such things appealed very little to him — but because it was one of the show places of England and had certain traditions that money could not buy. Before the weekend was over he had made an offer to his host to purchase the place, lock, stock and barrel, an offer that had been courteously but firmly declined.

Morgan Stenson, however, was not used to having his wishes thwarted. A month later he repeated his offer, with the same result, though this time there was less courtesy and more firmness in Lord Overstream's refusal.

From that moment Stenson set to work to acquire by foul means what he could not obtain by fair.

At the end of two years Overstream found himself in such financial difficulties that he was glad to sell the estate for half the amount that Stenson had offered him in the beginning. His ruin had been entirely brought about by the machinations of Morgan Stenson!

The soft note of a buzzer sounded. Stretching out his lean hand Stenson picked up one of the four telephones that stood near his elbow.

'Hello!' he called in a thin voice. 'All

right; come straight up.'

Dropping the instrument back on its rack, he flicked open a gold box, took out a long cigar, delicately removed the band and, placing it between his thin lips, lit it. Leaning back in his chair he sent a stream of smoke floating towards the ceiling. There was a scarcely audible tap at the door, and it opened to admit the obese figure of the bald-headed man. Closing the door behind him he advanced across the thick carpet to the desk.

'Sit down, Voles,' said Stenson, and when the other had taken the seat opposite him: 'What's your news?'

'We have searched the book thoroughly, Mr. Stenson,' said the stout man. 'There is nothing in it!'

The thin brows of the man before him drew together.

'Nothing?' he inquired.

The bald-headed man shook his head. 'Nothing!' he declared.

'But this fellow, Judge, didn't he tell you that was the book Jordan sent him?'

Voles nodded.

'So Muller said,' he said. 'He and

Casler forced it out of him at the point of the knife!'

'They should have made sure before they killed him,' he muttered. 'So far as I can see, the man fooled them.' His hooded eyes narrowed. 'This is the second time you've bungled in two days, Voles. I do not like people who make mistakes.'

'It's not my fault, Mr. Stenson!' protested the fat man.

'It is immaterial to me whose fault it is!' snapped Stenson curtly. 'You had your instructions, and you should see that the people you employ are capable of carrying them out. When Muller and Casler went that night to the vicarage they failed to take into consideration the fact that the man Dene had made a copy of the contents of the Prior's Key. It's the first thing I should have thought of. When you discovered who this man Dene was and sent Moreno to watch him, with instructions that he was to be removed, Moreno bungled matters, and now you tell me again that there has been a mistake. Surely you are capable of doing

133

the spade work?'

'I will see that you have no cause for future complaint,' Voles said.

'Do,' answered Stenson. 'And remember, Voles, these mistakes have got to be rectified. Dene is a dangerous man. I'm pretty sure at the moment that he knows nothing definite concerning the plan. If he did he would not be wasting his time trying to discover Jordan's statement. He must never find it! You are having him watched?'

Voles nodded.

'Good! Arrange that he is not lost track of for one instant, and at the first available opportunity see that he is rendered harmless! The early editions of the evening newspaper carry an account of the affair of the Aeolian Harp, and Dene will guess its significance. Unless I am very much mistaken he will go down to the place to make his own investigations. See if something cannot be done there. Now, what about the girl?'

'I have had very little opportunity to question her again,' said Voles. 'These other matters have occupied all my time, but I am under the impression that she knows nothing.'

'Make certain of that,' said Stenson. 'I don't mind to what lengths you go, but make definitely certain. In any case she must be kept a prisoner and closely guarded. I don't think you can do better than keep her at the cottage; being part of this estate, it is the safest place. It is a thousand pities that we should have had this trouble at practically the last moment. Everything else is going smoothly.'

'You will be ready by the twenty-seventh?' asked Voles, and Stenson nodded.

'I shall be ready by the twenty-seventh,' he answered. 'Li Fu leaves China on the thirtieth of this month. Von Beck will arrive from Germany on the tenth. Lenoir flies over from Paris on the twenty-second. Chase is due from America on the nineteenth, and Carillo arrives from Rome on the twenty-second. The final meeting will take place here at midnight on the twenty-seventh, and instructions will be issued to all our agents. Dostoviski is working night and day at the Yorkshire place to complete everything by then. I have allowed for everything, taken everything into consideration, and we cannot fail!'

'Your organisation has been marvellous,' admitted the stout man admiringly.

'There is only one danger,' said Stenson, removing the cigar from between his thin lips, 'and that is Dene. He must be eliminated, Voles! It is essential that you see to that!'

'I will,' answered Voles. 'Rest assured, Mr. Stenson, that you will have nothing to fear from Michael Dene.'

'Both him and these two men who are working with him!' insisted Stenson. 'It should not be difficult.'

The gentle purr of the buzzer broke the silence again as he stopped speaking, and Voles hoisted himself with difficulty out of the chair and picked up one of the receivers.

'Speaking,' he said softly, and listened for some time in silence. Then, covering the mouthpiece with a podgy hand, he looked at Stenson. 'The man Dene and his two companions have just left Claybury by car,' he announced. 'Have you any instructions?'

'Only that they must be followed,' said Stenson curtly.

'Garwin is following,' replied Voles. 'It was Bridger who rang up.'

'Unless I am mistaken.' murmured Stenson, 'they are on their way to the Aeolian Harp. Send Muller and Casler down there, Voles. The book containing the third section and the clue to the fourth is still at the inn. It must not fall into the hands of Dene, you understand?'

'I understand,' said Voles and, hanging up the receiver, crossed noiselessly to the door and went out, leaving Morgan Stenson to enjoy the rest of his cigar in peace.

16

The Fourth Clue

Michael Dene and his two companions reached Meopham as the slanting rays of the evening sun sent long shadows over the countryside. The Aeolian Harp was situated just outside the village, a picturesque building of white stone, standing in a bay at the side of a quiet country road and surrounded by a garden in which the roses blended with a profusion of old-world flowers to form a colourful setting for this ancient hostelry.

The figure of a uniformed policeman who stood on guard at the entrance struck an incongruous note, and was the only outward indication that death, in its most dreadful form, had stalked through that peace and beauty. As the Secret Service man brought the car to a stop and got down from the driving seat the constable approached.

'You can't stop here!' he said authorita-
tively. 'The place is closed until further
orders. There was a murder committed
here last night, and — '

'I'm aware of that!' broke in Dene. 'Is
your inspector about?'

'No, 'e ain't,' said the policeman.
'There's nobody about but me. Now you
get along. I've 'ad enough trouble already
with sightseers and reporters and — '

'Listen, my man,' interrupted Dene
again, and the note of authority in his
voice startled the constable. 'I'm neither a
reporter nor a sightseer. I'm here on
business in connection with this crime,
and I want to see your inspector as soon
as possible.'

'He's at the police station, sir,' said the
constable, a little bewildered at the appearance of this lean man who had been in no
way overawed by his official capacity. 'He's
got a conference with the Chief Constable,
I believe.'

'That's excellent!' said Dene. 'Where is
the police station?'

The man directed him, and getting
back into the car the Secret Service man

backed it, turned it skilfully in the narrow roadway, and set off in search of the police station. It was only a short drive and presently they drew up outside the rural red-brick building.

Leaving Peter and Colgate-Jones in the car, Dene entered the charge-room. A bucolic-looking sergeant was sitting at the desk, and to him Dene disclosed his identity and asked if he could see the inspector. 'He's in the office, sir,' said the sergeant, 'with Major Witherspoon. If you'll wait just a minute, sir, I'll tell him you want to see him.'

He got down laboriously from his stool, and, crossing to a door, tapped. Dene heard a muffled voice say gruffly: 'Come in,' and the sergeant entered, closing the door behind him. In less than five seconds he was out again.

'Come this way, sir, please,' he invited, and holding the door open ushered the Secret Service man into a small office in which two men were seated, occupying nearly the whole of the tiny apartment.

'Good evening, gentlemen,' said Dene pleasantly, looking from one to the other.

'I'm sorry to disturb you in the middle of an important conference, but my business is urgent. Your sergeant, of course, has told you who I am, and if you require further proof this ought to satisfy you.'

He took from his pocket the document he had shown to Colgate-Jones and handed it to the man behind the desk, who was obviously the representative of the local police. The inspector adjusted his steel-rimmed spectacles and studied the official warrant with slow deliberation. When he had finished he passed it to the grey-haired, dapper man who was sitting near him.

'Pleased to make your acquaintance, Mr. Dene,' he said heavily, 'though I can't think quite how the murder of poor Mr. Judge can have anything to do with the Secret Service.'

'That I am prepared to explain,' said Michael Dene.

'It appears this is a more serious matter than we realised, Hatch,' said the grey-haired man, handing the warrant back to Dene. 'I shall be interested to hear what you have to tell us, sir. This is

141

Inspector Hatch of the Gravesend Police, and my name is Witherspoon, Chief Constable of the county.'

Dene acknowledged the introduction.

'May I sit down?' he said, and without waiting for permission drew up a chair to the desk. 'I am engaged,' he began, 'on a very delicate inquiry — how delicate you will realise when I tell you that it concerns a plot against the welfare of Great Britain, and possibly the world.'

'You amaze me, Mr. Dene,' said Major Witherspoon, when he finally concluded. 'Naturally, I had no idea that anything so — so vast was at stake. We shall be only too glad to assist you in any way that lies in our power.'

'Thank you,' said the Secret Service man. 'First of all, I should like a detailed account of the circumstances surrounding the killing of Judge, and after that a permit to examine the premises on which the crime was committed.'

'Very well, sir,' said the inspector, and with admirable economy of words told the Secret Service man what he wanted to know.

Martin Judge had been a bachelor, and had bought the Aeolian Harp eleven years previously. He had lived there entirely alone, his personal wants being attended to by a woman who came daily from the village to cook his meals and do such cleaning as was necessary. The pot-man, who assisted in the bar, also lived in the village, arriving at seven o'clock in the morning and leaving after closing hours. It was this man who had discovered the crime.

He had arrived at the inn, as usual, to find the main door open, and had discovered Judge lying in a pool of blood in the middle of the taproom floor. The till had been broken open and the previous night's takings were missing. The murderer, or murderers, had left no clue behind, and the police had, until Dene's arrival, been under the impression that it was an ordinary case of robbery and murder.

'The breaking open of the till and the taking of the money was, of course, a blind,' declared Dene, when the inspector came to the end of his narrative. 'These people were after something of infinitely more importance, and I'm very much afraid they got it.'

He expressed a desire to go up to the inn at once, and with this Inspector Hatch and the Chief Constable concurred. Accompanying him out to the waiting car they were introduced to Peter and Colgate-Jones.

The distance between the police station and the inn was covered in record time by Dene's powerful car, and the constable on duty hurried forward as the machine came to a halt, and he saw his superiors alight.

'Everything all right, Cobb?' asked the inspector, as the constable saluted.

'Yes, sir,' answered Cobb. 'There ain't been nobody 'ere except this gentleman and one or two of the villagers snoopin' round. I soon sent them about their business,' he added, with satisfaction.

They passed under the low porch and entered a narrow passageway, panelled in black oak, across the ceiling of which ran beams of the same aged wood. On the right was an oblong opening, with a counter, through which they could see

144

shelves laden with bottles and glasses. To the left was an open doorway, giving admittance to a small room in which there were half a dozen tables and several chairs, and which, in a more pretentious establishment would probably be called the 'Saloon Lounge'. Facing this door was another, which was locked.

'This is the taproom,' said the inspector, taking a key from his pocket and thrusting it into the keyhole. 'The body, of course, has been removed, sir, but you can see the spot where it was found.'

He unlocked the door and entered, followed by Michael Dene and the Chief Constable; Peter and Colgate-Jones remaining outside.

The taproom was fairly large, with a sanded floor and panelled like the passageway and the other rooms. A dartboard hung against one wall, beside the bar, and in another corner was a little table. In the centre of the floor was an irregular brownish-red stain, which had soaked into the sawdust and mutely testified to the spot where Martin Judge had died.

Dene glanced keenly round, but he

could see nothing of interest. Innumerable people had been in this room since the murder, and any clue that might have been discovered in the sawdust had been obliterated by the tramping feet.

'I suppose you made a search of the dead man's belongings?' he inquired.

Inspector Hatch nodded.

'Yes, sir, we did that,' he answered, 'to see if anything else apart from the money had been stolen, but nothing had been disturbed.'

'Judge was rather a bookish man, wasn't he?' said Dene, and it was Major Witherspoon who answered.

'Yes,' he replied. 'He was a very well read and highly educated man. I think he bought this property more as a hobby than anything else.'

'Had he a large collection of books?' inquired the Secret Service man.

'More than you'd find in the average publican's possession, sir,' said Hatch. 'They're in his private sitting room. I'll show you if you're finished here.'

Dene took a last look round and joined the others at the door. Hatch came out and locked the door behind him, crossed the passage, and turned into another that ran at right angles behind the little lounge. Here he pushed open a door and the Secret Service man found himself looking into a pleasantly-furnished sitting room. The leaded windows were covered by chintz curtains; two comfortable armchairs, covered in the same material, were drawn up in front of the empty grate, and against one wall was a large oak bookcase that blended with the panelling, stuffed with volumes of all shapes and sizes.

The Secret Service man went over and examined it. He had little hope of discovering the book of which he was in search, the copy of Shakespeare in which, according to the rhyme, Norris Jordan had concealed the fourth clue. The men who had murdered Judge had certainly not gone without that.

A glance at the loaded shelves confirmed his supposition. There was no copy of Shakespeare to be seen, but there was a blank space on the second shelf — the only blank space in the bookcase.

'I suppose all the books he possessed

were in this room?' he asked, turning to the inspector. 'He didn't keep any anywhere else in the house?'

Hatch shook his head.

'No, sir,' he answered, 'except one. We found that in an envelope in one of the drawers of his dressing table in his bedroom. It was a copy of Shakespeare — '

He broke off at Dene's exclamation,

'Where is it?' demanded the Secret Service man. 'Here?'

'Yes, sir,' said the astonished inspector. 'We left it in the drawer.''

'Take me up to the bedroom at once!' snapped Dene, and his eyes gleamed. Had the people he was up against failed to secure what they wanted after all? Had they, in some extraordinary way, made a mistake and taken the wrong book?

These thoughts passed rapidly through his mind as he followed inspector Hatch up the narrow staircase to the floor above.

Martin Judge's bedroom was a large apartment with a sloping ceiling. It was sparsely furnished with a bed, a small table, a washstand and a chest of drawers that also did duty as a dressing table. The inspector crossed to this last piece of furniture, and pulling open the lowest drawer took out a large envelope.

'There's the book, sir,' he said, handing it to Dene, and eagerly the Secret Service man withdrew the volume from its wrappings.

It was a copy of Shakespeare's plays bound in limp suede leather. Rapidly Dene flicked over the pages. It was a new book, and from its appearance had not been much handled. Jordan's secret, if this was indeed the volume he hinted at in the rhyme, must be contained in the binding.

While Peter and Colgate-Jones watched him eagerly, the Secret Service man took a knife from his pocket and began to rip the leather to pieces.

'It seems a pity,' he murmured, almost apologetically, 'but it can't be helped.'

It was in the spine that he found what he was seeking, between the leather and the paper backing, the third strip of Norris Jordan's precious document. It was similar in size and shape to the other two, and contained the following words:

3.
my dea . . .
of my
is a
culminate
hind th . . .
ject is
uired
has
is to
ruining
mercy
r.
ears th . . .
of the..
mewhere
en abl . . .
e country
ard an . . .
the si . . .
dolf vo . . .
nd Morg . . .
of the
eeting o . . .
Stel W . . .
I am
ore th . . .

t in ca . . .
I have

Inwardly excited but outwardly calm, Michael Dene took his wallet from his pocket and extracted the two sections he had already in his possession. Going over to the table he laid them down side by side and fitted number three into its place. Leaning over his shoulder, Peter and Colgate-Jones read the result:

1. 2. 3.
In case of my dea . . .
the result of my
years. There is a
which will culminate
The people behind th . . .
men whose object is
They have acquired
invention which has
their intention is to
reserve, thus ruining
it at the mercy
the event of war.
For fifteen years th . . .

gold reserve of the . . .
a place somewhere
have not been abl . . .
and when the country
to come forward an . . .
The names of the si . . .
Paul Lenoir, Adolf vo . . .
Wu Li Fu and Morg . . .
the organiser of the
The final meeting o . . .
July 27th at Stel W . . .
Buckinghamshire. I am
evidence before th . . .
this plot, but in ca . . .
being able to I have

'It takes us a little further,' said the Secret Service man. 'It's obvious from this that Jordan noted down all the names of the people concerned in the con-spiracy. The final meeting, which takes place on July 27th at Stel-something, is in Buckinghamshire.'

He turned the strip which he had taken from the book cover and discovered the inevitable rhyme on the back.

'The lowest value in a game of skill,
And what is talked by men who use
  the quill.
Next a bird of habitation, choose the
  right,
In a sacred edifice of snowy white.'

'They get worse!' grunted Peter. 'What
the dickens is one to make of that?'

'We'll see what we can do with it later,'
said Dene, as he folded the three slips
and put them carefully in his pocket
book. 'In the meantime we have something of more importance to attend to.'

Colgate-Jones raised his eyebrows.

'More importance?' he said doubtfully.

Michael Dene nodded. 'Yes,' he answered.
'These people killed Judge last night and
got away with the wrong book. It won't be
long before they find out their mistake
and take steps to rectify it. Nothing is
more certain, in my opinion, than that
they'll come back here to try to retrieve
their error. Our job is to see that they
don't get away again.'

17

The Escape

It seemed to Mary Jordan, lying uncomfortably on the damp floor of the dingy and grimy kitchen, that she had been in this unpleasant place for ages. Since the sensation caused by the mention of Michael Dene's name she had seen nothing of the bald-headed man. A hard-faced woman had brought her food at intervals, but no one else had come near her.

She had tried to engage this unpleasant female in conversation but without result. She steadfastly refused to answer any questions, and confined her remarks to monosyllabic interjections. Her appearances only took place at long intervals, and then she stayed for a very short time. Mary was under the impression that when she left, the cottage was tenantless, except for herself, and it was this that suggested to her the possibility of escape.

Her hard-faced gaoler had just paid one of her intermittent visits, bringing her a cup of weak, over-sweet tea and thick slabs of bread and butter, and there would be a long period before she came again. Mary, her eyes on the grimy ceiling, racked her brains to try to think of a practical means for getting out of her unpleasant position.

She was a great reader, and in her favourite novels the heroines were always finding themselves in a similar predicament. Unfortunately, in her place there was none of the possible means of escape, which in her fictional counterparts had been so thoughtfully provided by the author. If she could once get free of her bonds, the outlook would be less difficult. It would surely be possible to find some means of getting out of that room.

She concentrated on this problem, and her heart sank when, after what must have been the greater part of two hours, she had to admit that she could think of no practical method. She closed her eyes for a moment and rested her weary brain, and then, as sometimes happens, her sub-conscious mind supplied what her conscious mind had failed to do.

A hazy, nebulous idea began to form itself. A vague recollection of something she had read came seeping up out of the lumber room of her memory. She was unable to tell where or in what circum-stances she had seen it, but the incident gradually grew clear and well-defined. Sometime, somewhere, in a book she could not recall, she had read of a girl who had found herself in a situation similar to her own, and she remembered how that girl had succeeded in getting free. A surge of hope came flooding back to wash away her despair.

Without further loss of time she began to put her Heaven-sent plan into execution. Drawing up her knees and straightening them again, she was able to push herself along over the stone-paved floor, and in this caterpillar fashion she worked her way towards the great open fireplace with its rusty kitchen range. It took her some time, for her progress was necessarily slow, but presently she found herself, bruised and breathless, lying close up against the mass of broken metal which constituted the remains of the kitchen stove.

For a second or two she lay still to recover from her exertions, and then began to carry out the second part of her scheme. With difficulty she twisted until her bound wrists were pressing against the rough edge of the broken plate shelf below the oven door, which had been her objective. She had noticed it was broken when her great idea first came to her. After some little difficulty she succeeded in getting the cords in contact with the sharp edge and laboriously began to rub them backwards and forwards.

Her arms were aching with the unnatural position she had to maintain, and the perspiration was pouring down her face as she felt one of the cords give. She could have cried aloud with delight. Her plan had been successful!

She forced her wrists apart and felt the confining bonds loosened. A moment later her hands were free!

She paused for a little while to recover

from her efforts, and then, sitting up, set about untying her ankles. Her previous endeavours to free herself had tightened the knots, and she found difficulty in undoing them. She managed at last, however, with no worse casualty than a broken fingernail, and gasped with relief when she found herself free.

The pain, as the restored circulation began to flow once more, was excruciating, but she set her teeth and waited for it to pass off. In a moment or two it did so, and she struggled shakily to her feet. A wave of dizziness overcame her, and she had to clutch at the mantelpiece for support, but this, too, was only momentary, and then her head cleared and she looked about her.

Her next task was to find some means of getting out of this horrible room. Going over, she tried the door through which the bald-headed man had entered, but it was locked, and she had expected nothing more. Neither was she disappointed when she discovered that the door, which she concluded gave admittance to the scullery, was also tightly fastened. She turned her attention to the window. The aged wooden shutters had been closed across this and were held in place by a thick piece of timber screwed into the window frame. If only she had a screwdriver, she thought, it would be easy; the screws were new and would have offered little opposition. With only her fingers, however, they were as immovable as steel bars sunk in solid concrete.

It occurred to her that possibly she might find something that would loosen the screws among the odds and ends in the kitchen. The dresser was cluttered up with a collection of dirty and broken crockery, and she found nothing here that was likely to help her. There were three drawers in the lower part of the structure, and these she pulled open, rummaging among their contents.

For the most part they held a collection of odd pieces of string, ragged, mildewed dusters, tin lids, and a general collection of rubbish that had accumulated during the occupation of the last tenant. She found nothing, however, that even suggested a means of loosening those screws that rendered the window impassable.

Disappointed, and with her hopes that had been so high rather dashed, she sat on the edge of the table and with wrinkled brows tried to think a way out of her difficulty. If only there had been a knife she could have used the blade as an improvised tool to loosen those screws.

A sudden thought struck her. Perhaps the kitchen range that had already proved such good service would yield something. She went over and inspected it, carrying the smoky lamp with her, but at first glance there was nothing here either that was likely to assist her. She was turning away to set the lamp back on the table when it occurred to her to open the oven door. The heavy piece of metal swung back on its rusty hinges and she peered into the interior.

It contained nothing but an old iron saucepan, the broken handle of which lay on the iron shelf beside it, but it was sufficient to cause her to utter an exclamation of delight. Here was something that might be utilised for a screwdriver. Picking up the iron handle she carried it back with the lamp to the table and examined it. It had been broken off where it had been riveted on to the saucepan and the other end was square and flat. She tried it on one of the screws, but it was too thick to fit the slot. Biting her lips she considered what to do next.

If only the end had been thinner it would have been ideal. Was there any possible way by which it could be ground down? The concrete slab on which the old stove stood caught her eye and supplied the answer. Hurriedly she went over, and kneeling down, began to scrape the end of the metal bar on the rough substance.

It took her some time, and necessitated frequent journeys to the window to test her progress, but eventually she had in her possession a very fair improvised screwdriver.

She tried it on the first screw, her heart in her mouth. It acted perfectly and in a few minutes the screw was out and lying on the table beside her, and she had started on the second.

Her hands were sore and her wrists ached before the last screw was out but she was triumphant. She had succeeded!

Laying the heavy wooden box aside she pulled at the shutters, and they swung back, revealing the grimy glass of the window behind. It was pitch dark outside and she could hear the sound of heavy rain. She was rather surprised to discover it was night, for she had lost all sense of time — a glance at her watch after she had freed her hands had shown her that it had stopped — but she cared little whether it was night or day, darkness or light, all that mattered to her was that before her lay freedom!

Cautiously she eased the window up inch by inch until there was sufficient room for her to squeeze through. A moment later she was standing knee deep in wet, rank undergrowth outside the house!

Now that she was free a sudden panic took possession of her, the horrible fear that she would be caught and dragged back to that unpleasant prison place before she could get away. It lent wings to her feet and sent her stumbling frantically through the rain, heedless of her direction, heedless of anything, except to put as big a distance as possible between herself and the sinister cottage in which she had been kept prisoner.

Quite suddenly she came to a thick hedge. It loomed up out of the darkness almost before she was aware of its presence, and she realized that it marked the boundary of the cottage garden. She was forced to pause and seek some outlet, for the hedge grew too thickly to force a passage through it. Following its course, searching for a break, she reached the dilapidated gate through which she had been carried. It was fastened with a chain and padlock, but she managed to scramble over, and reaching the other side, ran as hard as she could for the shelter of the wood. Once she was among the thickly growing trees she felt safer and checked her pace.

It was pitch dark here and she had to move warily to avoid the clustered trunks; she could scarcely see a foot ahead, but she welcomed the darkness, for it offered a cloak of concealment against the possibility of pursuit. Not that there seemed any danger of this. The people who had taken her from the vicarage were as yet unaware that she had escaped; were unlikely to realize this until the woman made her morning visit. At the same time, there might be someone lurking in the vicinity of the cottage, and she had no desire to fall into their hands again.

For a long time afterwards Mary remembered that journey through the darkness of the wood. The pattern of the rain and the rustle of the undergrowth as some animal, disturbed by her approach, scurried for safety, were the only sounds that broke the stillness. She could hear the thumping of her heart as she stumbled on, wondering how much farther the forest extended. In the ordinary course of events she would have been terrified at finding herself in this lonely place at so late an hour, but all she experienced was intense relief at having once more regained her freedom. The darkness and the hidden dangers of the forest were as nothing compared with the fear that the bald-headed man had instilled in her.

Presently the trees began to thin, and

eventually she came out into a narrow lane. She was breathless and tired, her eyelids as heavy as lead, and for a moment she leaned against a wet tree trunk to consider what she should do next. She had no idea where she was except that it was somewhere in the heart of the country, but she concluded that if she kept on walking, sooner or later she would come to a town or village, and from there would be able to find some form of conveyance to take her back to the vicarage.

After a short rest she set off along the winding lane. It twisted and turned and she was beginning to think it would never end when she rounded a bend and came abruptly to a broad highway.

Here she paused again, wondering whether to turn to the right or left. It seemed to be immaterial since she had no idea where either way led, and she elected to turn to the right.

Her legs were beginning to feel as though they were made of lead, and each step began to get more difficult than the last. She found herself nodding as she walked and had to rouse herself with an effort. She would have given almost anything she possessed to have been able to lie down and sleep, but the fear that was still within her forced her onwards. She was soaked to the skin, and her wet hair hung in lank streaks, which clung to her cheeks.

It seemed to her that she had been walking for miles before the road began to slope sharply downhill, and she saw ahead of her a dim light. It grew brighter, and she realized that it was moving towards her. It came nearer, wavering in a peculiar manner that troubled her until she realized that it was attached to a bicycle. Here was help, and with a little sob of thankfulness she stepped out into the roadway to intercept the rider, and at that moment her strength gave out.

The light danced frantically before her eyes, she swayed, tried to recover herself, and collapsed in a limp heap in the wet road.

18

The Fight at the Inn

The man who lay along the branch of the big oak tree overlooking the road that passed the entrance to the Aeolian Harp moved slightly to ease his cramped limbs. He had been there since darkness had fallen and he was wet and uncomfortable. With the coming of sunset heavy rainclouds had blown up from the west, and from dusk onwards it had rained unceasingly.

The night was very quiet, and from somewhere in the neighbouring village a clock struck the hour, a single stroke that vibrated to silence.

Faintly to his ears came the whine of a car, and away in the distance he saw through his glasses a momentary gleam of light. It vanished and the noise ceased; once again there was silence, but now he kept his eyes glued to the stretch of road

167

that from his position was visible for several hundred yards.

Ten minutes passed, and then vaguely he made out the dim figures of men approaching, seven shadowy shapes that moved noiselessly towards the tree in which he lay concealed. They came cautiously, these sinister shapes bred of the night, moving with a stealthy soundlessness that was uncanny. The watcher put away his glasses and began to descend the tree. He reached the ground and stood waiting in the shelter of a hedge. The hoot of an owl came to his ears, and pursing his lips he gave vent to an answering call, and after a slight pause the first of the approaching figures joined him. He was dressed in black that made him almost invisible in the darkness.

'Is everything all right?' he whispered in a muffled tone — muffled because he spoke through the silk that covered his face.

'Yes,' replied the watcher. 'The place is deserted.'

The other six, similarly dressed and masked, had come up with the first man and stood listening.

'Where is the man Dene?' whispered the one who had spoken before.

'Gone to the hotel in the village,' was the reply.

'And he found nothing? You're sure he found nothing, Steffson?'

The watcher shook his head.

'He brought nothing out of the place with him!' he declared.

'Then the book is still there,' said the other, a note of satisfaction in his voice. 'That is good. The man Judge fooled us, but we will rectify our error. Let's start; the quicker we begin the longer we shall have to complete our task before daylight comes.'

He led the way across the road, followed by his seven companions. Noiselessly, keeping in the shadow of the hedge, he approached the bay in which the deserted inn stood, and presently came to a halt under the porch at the entrance. There was the faint clink of metal against metal, a long pause, and the sharp crack of splintering wood. The door swung inwards, and the sinister host melted into the blackness of the passage-way beyond. The door closed behind the last man and a beam of light sprang to life. It came from a torch held in one of the intruders' hands. It wavered over the dark panelling and finally settled, a circle of vague radiance, on the bend in the passage.

'It's the sitting room we want,' whispered the man who had spoken to Steffson, 'that's where the books are. We'll try that first, and if we can't find what we want there we'll search the rest of the house.'

Cautiously the group of black figures advanced, the man with the torch lighting the way. He paused again at the door of the room in which Martin Judge, during his lifetime, had spent so many pleasant hours. It was unlocked, and pushing it open they entered.

The light of the torch went dancing round the apartment, and presently came to rest on the laden bookcases. The man who was apparently in charge of the expedition turned to his companions.

'Three of us will be sufficient to

conduct the search,' he whispered. 'The rest of you keep guard, front and back, there may be a police patrol that comes round at intervals.'

Four of the men withdrew and the others, working swiftly, began to examine the contents of the bookcase. It did not take them very long, and when they had finished their leader uttered an exclamation of disappointment.

'It is not here,' he muttered. 'We must look elsewhere.'

They left the sitting room and came out into the passage.

'Let us try the man's bedroom, perhaps it is there,' came the whispered suggestion, and noiselessly they began to ascend the narrow staircase.

Into the dark and silent room which the dead man had occupied they crept, and the torch was flashed this way and that, picking out the various articles of furniture. A built-in cupboard occupied their attention for a moment, but they soon discovered that this contained nothing but clothes.

'The chest of drawers,' said the man in

charge below his breath. 'Try that.'

They pulled out the receptacles, one after the other, and one of them uttered a low cry of triumph as, in the lowest drawer, he came upon a book.

'Is this it?' he muttered, passing it over to the leader.

The man snatched it eagerly and examined it in the ray of the torch.

'This must be it,' he said. 'See, it's a volume of Shakespeare. We'll make quite certain this time, though, before we leave!'

'I don't think you'll have an opportunity,' said a cool voice from the doorway, and with a muttered oath the man swung round, his hand flying to the pocket of his long coat. 'Keep still!' snapped the voice sharply. 'I've got a pistol in my hand and if you move I shall shoot! I don't want another experience of your gas bombs.'

'Michael Dene!' breathed Steffson.

'Quite right,' said the Secret Service man, coming into the room, and from behind him came a beam of light that focussed itself on the startled marauders. 'I'm afraid you've been just a little bit too clever. I found the real book earlier this evening, but I guessed you might be coming, and as I didn't want to disappoint you I obtained a copy of Shakespeare and left it for you to find. Up with your hands, all of you!' His voice grew stem. 'The place is surrounded and you have no chance of getting away.'

Slowly the black-clad figures raised their arms.

'That's better,' said Dene, and without turning his head spoke to someone in the shadows behind him. 'Go and search them,' he said.

Peter and Colgate-Jones came into the light from the blackness of the passage, and being careful to keep out of the line of fire, crossed over to the cornered men and began to run through their pockets.

Michael Dene was so intent in watching this proceeding, alert for the slightest attempt on the part of the three to try and take them by surprise that he failed to hear the faint sound made by the creeping shape that was coming stealthily up behind him.

The first warning he got of danger was

when a gloved hand reached out and gripped his pistol wrist, while at the same time a strong arm was flung around his neck and a hard knee ground into the small of his back. As he was jerked off his balance his trigger finger involuntarily pressed the trigger and the little automatic belched fire and death. The noise was deafening in the confined space of the bedroom, but the bullets buried themselves harmlessly in the ceiling.

At the same instant the others became aware of what had happened, and flung themselves on Colgate-Jones and Peter. Taken by surprise they staggered backwards. Peter tripped over the edge of a rug and fell with a crash, his assailant on top of him. Colgate-Jones managed to keep his balance. The man who had attacked him aimed a vicious blow at his head, but the clergyman skilfully sidestepped and swung a vicious right, which caught his opponent below the ear and sent him reeling away with a singing head. The days of his youth, when he had been one of the finest amateur boxers in the country, were standing Colgate-Jones in good stead. With a grunt of delight he looked round for fresh worlds to conquer.

Steffson came at him like a whirlwind, an ugly-looking knife clasped in his right hand. Colgate-Jones waited for him coolly, and as he lunged with the weapon, ducked to one side and brought the edge of his palm down with all his force on the man's wrist. Steffson gave a sharp cry of pain, the knife dropped from his hand and stuck quivering in the floor.

The clergyman followed up his advantage. Like a piston rod his arm shot out and his bunched fist caught the other on the point of the jaw. As he staggered back Colgate-Jones' left came up under his chin. He crumpled up with a grunt, and breathing a little harder the clergyman swung round to meet the other man who had recovered from the blow on his ear. They clinched, and went staggering backwards and forwards, fighting desperately.

Peter, in the meanwhile, was having a rough time. His opponent seemed possessed of abnormal strength, and the advantage he had gained at the start he had managed to maintain, in spite of all Peter's efforts to throw him off. His hands had fastened themselves on Peter's throat with a grip that was like a vice, and try as he would he couldn't dislodge that stranglehold. The result might have gone hard with him if Michael Dene, who had succeeded temporarily in freeing himself from his assailant, had not seen what was happening and come to his rescue.

The Secret Service man still retained his automatic, and he brought the butt of this down with all his force on the stranger's head. The man collapsed without a sound, his grip on Peter's throat relaxing. Peter got painfully to his feet.

'Thanks,' he said hoarsely, and went to the assistance of Colgate-Jones.

He had just succeeded in hauling the man off the vicar when a warning cry from Dene drew his attention to the door. Four other black-clad figures came in with a concerted rush, and a moment later they were fighting furiously against odds.

It was impossible now to tell friend

from foe. Lashing out wildly the Secret Service man felt his fist connect with a hard chin, heard a grunt of pain, and then a flash of orange flame and an ear-slitting report as a pistol was fired almost in his face. The wind of the bullet stirred his hair as it whistled perilously close to his head. A hand gripped his ankle and jerked him off his feet. He fell with a crash, striking the back of his head on the floor.

Half a dozen uniformed men came pouring through the open doorway, and after that the fight became more evenly matched. Armed only with their truncheons the policemen battered down the defences of the intruders, and a short while after their appearance on the scene it was all over. But their victory had not been established without casualties. One of the policemen had a bullet through his leg; another's tunic was ripped to rags by the razor sharp blade of the knife with which he had been attacked.

Michael Dene, his arm numb and painful, surveyed the eight prisoners with satisfaction.

'A good night's work,' he remarked. 'They're only pawns, but they're worth capturing all the same.'

Colgate-Jones uttered an exclamation.

'You've got it, Dene!' he cried. 'You've got it!'

The Secret Service man looked at him in surprise.

'Got what?' he asked.

'The solution of Jordan's rhyme!' said Colgate-Jones excitedly.

' "The lowest value in a game of skill'. A pawn is the lowest value in chess!'

'And what is talked by men who use the quill?' put in Peter, speaking with difficulty through swollen lips. 'Shop, of course. All writers, when they get together, talk 'shop'!'

Dene nodded, his eyes gleaming.

'Which gives us 'pawnshop',' he said softly. 'The fourth section of Jordan's document is in a pawnshop — somewhere.'

19

Startling News

It was a battered and weary party that made their way to Gravesend in the small hours of the morning. Peter's lips were sore and swollen and one of Colgate-Jones' eyes was rapidly turning black. The wound in Michael Dene's arm was not severe but painful. The bullet had grazed the fleshy part, and although it had bled freely, little or no damage had been done. One of the policemen had dressed it roughly, and when they reached the station house it was attended to properly by the Divisional Surgeon, who, luckily, had been called from his bed to attend to a case of drunkenness.

The prisoners were marshalled in the charge-room and questioned, but nothing could be got out of them. They refused to say anything, maintaining a sullen silence. They were charged with 'breaking and entering' and sent down to the cells.

'And,' said the sergeant in charge as they were led away, 'we shall 'ave difficulty in findin' room for 'em. This place was never built to accommodate a h'army.'

There was nothing Dene could do, and after he, Peter and Colgate-Jones had accepted the hot coffee, which Major Witherspoon had ordered on their arrival, they took leave of the Chief Constable and set off for the vicarage in Dene's car.

They were all thoroughly tired out. The long day and the strenuous night had left them weary and longing for sleep, but sleep was not to be vouchsafed to them for some time. They arrived at Colgate-Jones' house by the river in the grey light of early morning, and to their surprise were greeted by Mrs. Sutherland. The housekeeper was only partially dressed and appeared to be labouring under great excitement.

'I'm so glad you've got back, sir,' she greeted the vicar breathlessly. 'The young lady's returned.'

'What?' exclaimed Colgate-Jones, and

Peter echoed, 'Returned? When did she come back?'

'About two hours ago,' replied the housekeeper. 'I was in bed and asleep. She was brought back by a policeman.'

'Where is she now?' demanded Michael Dene.

'In bed and asleep,' answered Mrs. Sutherland. 'I thought it was the best place for her. She was exhausted, poor dear, she could scarcely stand.'

'Thank Heaven!' muttered Peter. 'Thank Heaven she's safe.'

Dene was frowning thoughtfully.

'She must have succeeded in escaping,' he said. 'They'd never have let her go. I wonder if she'll be able to tell us anything?'

'You can't disturb her now,' said Mrs. Sutherland. 'The best thing she can do is to sleep as long as possible.'

'I'd no intention of disturbing her,' said the Secret Service man. 'I was only wondering if she would be able to help us when she woke.'

So far as any vital information was concerned he was to be disappointed. The morning was well advanced, a warm, sunny morning with a clear blue sky, when he woke from a long refreshing sleep, had a bath, shaved and dressed himself and went down to find the girl sitting on the little lawn that sloped to the river.

She looked pale and wan, but the rest had done her good and in answer to Dene's questions she related all that had happened to her since her abduction from the vicarage.

'When I recovered consciousness,' she concluded, 'after I fainted in the roadway, I found a policeman bending over me. It was a cyclist patrol and it had been the light of his bicycle that I had seen. I told him who I was, and he took me to the police station, where the sergeant's wife gave me food and hot coffee. They seemed to know all about me there.' She smiled. 'Apparently my description had been circulated and they had been searching for me. When I had sufficiently recovered they questioned me, made me sign a statement, and sent me home.'

'I think you're remarkably lucky,'

commented Michael Dene.

'I think I am, too,' said the girl. 'If you'd seen that horrible place and that dreadful man — ' She shivered as her memory conjured up a vivid picture of the bald-headed Voles.

'I hope to have the pleasure of meeting the gentleman you mention very soon,' said Dene grimly. 'Now, Miss Jordan, have you any idea of the locality of this cottage to which you were taken?'

She shook her head.

'Except that it must be somewhere near Stoneham I have no idea,' she answered. 'I seemed to have walked miles before I met the policeman, but Stoneham was the name of the village that he took me to, it's a few miles outside Aylesbury.'

'Aylesbury,' murmured. Dene, and remembered the mention of Buckinghamshire, which occurred in the sections of Jordan's report which were already in his possession. 'It shouldn't be difficult to find,' he continued. 'A search of the surrounding districts ought to locate it easily.'

Colgate-Jones joined them at that moment, and for his edification the girl repeated what she had just told Dene. The clergyman's genial face was stern as he listened.

'Those people deserve horse-whipping for the way you were treated,' he said, 'and I'd like to be the one to do it.'

'You've done quite enough for the present,' said Dene, glancing at the purple surround that disfigured their host's right eye.

Colgate-Jones grinned.

'I haven't started yet,' he declared, 'and I have no intention of backing out now just when I'm beginning to enjoy myself! Here's Clayton.'

Mary's eyes widened.

'Clayton?' she echoed. 'But — surely — surely — isn't that the name of the man who — who killed my brother?'

Michael Dene shook his head.

'No, Miss Jordan,' he replied. 'Clayton had nothing to do with the death of your brother. The people responsible for that are the same people who kept you prisoner in that cottage — '

She looked from one to the other helplessly.

'I don't understand,' she said. 'What is it all about?'

'So far as that goes,' said the Secret Service man, 'I'm afraid I can't tell you, but I'm willing to tell you all that we know.'

He did so briefly, and she listened, her eyes growing wider in amazement as he proceeded.

At this moment Mrs. Sutherland appeared from the house to announce that breakfast was ready, and they made their way to the dining room to the late but welcome meal.

'The first two lines,' said Dene, when they were seated at the table and continuing the conversation, 'obviously give us a pawnshop, and the last two must supply us with the locality.'

'How do they go?' asked Peter, passing toast to Mary. Dene took his wallet from his pocket, extracted the slip, and laid it beside his plate.

'The whole rhyme runs: 'The lowest value in a game of skill, and what is talked by men who use the quill. Next a bird of habitation, choose the right, in a sacred edifice of snowy-white.' The first line as Colgate-Jones cleverly discovered, refers to a pawn, and the second, as you suggested, is obviously 'shop.' What we've got to find is the meaning of 'Next a bird of habitation, choose the right, in a sacred edifice of snowy white'.'

'A bird of habitation,' murmured Peter, and shook his head. 'I'm afraid that's got me.'

'Let's think of some birds' names,' mumbled Colgate-Jones, his mouth full of egg and bacon. 'There's the Lark, the Thrush, Crow, the Tit, the Starling, the Pigeon — that's all I can think of for the moment.'

'There's the Sparrow,' put in Peter, 'but that obviously can't mean a habitation. Can anyone think of any others?'

'There's the Swan and the Rook,' said the girl.

'The same thing applies,' said Colgate-Jones. 'Neither the Swan or the Rook suggests a house.'

'Doesn't it, though?' said Dene. 'I believe you've hit on it, Miss Jordan. The Rook, that's the bird we want.'

Peter looked at him, his face puzzled.

'Where do you get the habitation?' he asked.

'Remember how the rhyme starts?' asked Dene. ' "The lowest value in a game of skill" is a pawn. A Rook in the same game is also known as a castle. 'A bird of habitation,' you see?'

'By Jove, you're right!' said the vicar excitedly. 'The question is, which is it?'

'That probably depends on the last line,' said Dene. ' "In a sacred edifice of snowy white." A sacred edifice could mean a temple or church — '

'Or a chapel,' finished the clergyman, and Peter gave a cry of triumph.

'That's exactly what it does mean,' he said. 'White Chapel! We've got it! Jordan's fourth section is in a pawnshop next to a castle in Whitechapel!'

Michael Dene smiled.

'Naturally it doesn't refer to the kind of castle you're thinking of,' he answered. 'But 'The Castle' is a fairly common name for a public house.'

'You are at liberty to kick me,' said Peter calmly, reaching for a piece of toast.

'I ought to have thought of that.'

'It doesn't matter who thought of it,' said Colgate-Jones, 'the only thing that matters is that we've solved the rhyme. What's the next move?'

'A visit to the pawnshop, obviously,' said Dene. 'I'll ring up the police station in Whitechapel and ask them if they can give up the exact locality of the public house called 'The Castle,' next door to which is a pawnshop, and then — '

He broke off as the shrill summons of the telephone bell came to their ears.

'Excuse me,' said Colgate-Jones, and rising to his feet, left the dining room. He was back in a few minutes. 'The Gravesend police want to speak to you,' he announced.

'Most likely they've got those fellows to talk,' said Peter, as Dene crossed to the door. The Secret Service man had left the vicarage telephone number with the sergeant-in-charge in case they wished to communicate with him.

'Let's hope so,' said Dene, and went in search of the instrument.

He was away for nearly ten minutes.

When he came back his voice was grave.

'They haven't talked,' he said, 'and neither is there any likelihood of them doing so.'

'Why? What's happened?' demanded Colgate-Jones.

'They've escaped!' said the Secret Service man briefly. 'Half an hour ago a car containing eight men drew up at the police station and held up everyone in the place at the point of pistols. They were forced to unlock the cell doors and release the fellows we captured last night!' He gave a hard, quick laugh. 'They're the kind of people we're up against!' he said bitterly. 'I don't mind telling you that if we come out of this business alive we shall be very lucky!'

20

The Pawnshop

Mr. Aaron Rosenburg sat in a dingy, poky little office at the back of his equally dingy shop and gazed through the grimy panes of the small window facing his desk at the blurred view of the backyard, which constituted the unsavoury outlook to his domain.

The office was gloomy and ill-lighted, the paper faded, and the paintwork greasy. It had been old when Mr. Rosenburg's father as a young man had bought the business, and had been untouched from that day to this, but in spite of its unprepossessing appearance large sums of money had been made, and the old-fashioned safe which stood in one corner could have told stories of many thousands of pounds that had passed in and out of its worn interior. For the little pawnshop that stood next to the Castle in a side street off Whitechapel Road did a thriving business, and never had times been so good as they were at present.

Occasionally a stranger might enter the shop and offer something more pretentious in exchange for a larger loan, but Mr. Rosenburg preferred his regular clients. They paid him better, and there was no danger.

He remembered, with an uneasiness that always recurred to him when he thought of it, the diamond ring which had once been brought to him and on which he had advanced ten pounds, only to discover that it had been stolen property. Since that time Mr. Rosenburg had been very wary.

He closed his passbook and locked it away in a drawer of his desk with a sigh of satisfaction. Things were very good, very good indeed, he reflected as he leaned back in his chair and stroked his straggling grey beard.

He had every reason to be satisfied, and he deserved his success, for he was a kind man. There were many people in that teeming district who had cause to thank him for many little acts of benevolence. His bent figure in its shabby clothes was a familiar one on the Whitechapel Road. Punctually every morning, half an hour before the shop opened, he would take his daily constitutional, always covering the same ground and never deviating in his route, pausing every now and again to exchange a word with an acquaintance or pat the head of a small child hurrying on its way to school. A kind old man, but a hard bargainer in business as those who had attempted to get the better of him discovered to their cost.

The door opened and his wife came in, carrying the glass of milk and buttered scone, which invariably made up his lunch. She was a stout woman, with features that still showed something of the beauty that the years had almost wiped away.

'Busy this morning, Aaron?' she asked, as she set the plate and glass down at his side.

'Fairly, my dear,' he answered, in his thin, rather quavering voice. 'How is Rachel?'

'She is better, I think,' said his wife. 'She has eaten a little chicken.'

'Poor Rachel,' said the old man, shaking his head. 'It is now many years since Solly was killed, but she will never get over it. War is a terrible thing, a dreadful, stupid thing, which does no good to anyone.'

He was thinking of his son-in-law who had died two days before the Armistice.

'She had never been the same since,' said his wife.

'Can you wonder,' said old Aaron, spreading his hands. 'And war is in the air again, my dear. War, and death and destruction.'

There came a tap at the door and his spectacled clerk intruded a head.

'There's a gentleman to see you, Mr. Rosenburg,' he announced.

'A gentleman?' said the old Jew. 'What does he want?'

The clerk shook his head.

'I don't know,' he answered. 'He said he wished to see you on important business. Here is his card.'

Mrs. Rosenburg took it from his hand

and passed it to her husband. Old Aaron surveyed it with his keen, black eyes, as keen now as they had been thirty years previously.

'I do not know anyone of the name of Dene,' he muttered. 'What does he want? To pawn something?'

'I don't think so,' said the clerk. 'He came in a large car, a beautiful car.'

'That means nothing,' said his experienced employer. 'Ask him to come in.'

The clerk disappeared through the narrow passage that led to the shop, and Mrs. Rosenburg returned to her domain upstairs.

As Michael Dene was shown into the dingy office old Aaron turned in his swivelling chair.

'For why did you wish to see me?' he inquired.

'On a matter of business connected with a mutual friend of ours,' said the Secret Service man. 'I believe you were acquainted with a man called Norris Jordan.'

'That is so,' said Mr. Rosenburg, nodding his head slowly. 'Mr. Jordan and

I were friends. He was a man of great knowledge, a well-travelled man.'

'I have reason to believe,' continued Dene, 'that a few months ago he sent you a certain object to hold in trust for him until he should claim it or send someone with his authority. Is that correct?'

The old Jew hesitated, and Dene was under the impression that the keen eyes in the wrinkled face were summing him up.

'That is correct, Mr. Dene,' he answered, after a pause. 'Have you come to claim that object?'

'I have,' said the Secret Service man, inclining his head.

'I read in the newspapers,' went on old Aaron, his eyes still fixed steadily on Michael Dene's face, 'that my friend, Norris Jordan, met his death at the hands of a murderer. Has this object which you seek anything to do with that abominable crime?'

'It has everything to do with it,' answered Dene. 'You knew Jordan rather well, I take it?'

'Very well,' said the old man, and there

was a note of sorrow in his voice. 'Very well indeed. Mr. Jordan and I were friends, great friends. At a time when sorrow weighed heavily upon myself and my family he was most kind.'

'Then you will no doubt be aware,' continued the Secret Service man, 'that he dabbled, to a large extent, in politics.'

'I am aware of that,' said Aaron. 'Was his death, then, of political importance?'

'Yes,' answered Dene. 'He died because he had discovered a secret that was inimical to the safety of Britain.'

There was a moment's silence.

'How am I to know,' said the old Jew at last, 'that I do right by giving you this object which poor Jordan left in my care? How am I to know that you are the right man who has the authority to ask for it?'

For answer the Secret Service man produced his credentials, and the other examined them carefully.

'You have satisfied me,' he said, returning the papers. 'Just one minute, Mr. Dene.'

He rose to his feet, took a bunch of keys from his pocket, and crossing to the safe opened the door. From its interior he produced a small, cedar-wood box with a sliding lid. Bringing this back to the desk he slid the lid open and took out a large ivory chessman.

Although something of a connoisseur of carved ivory Dene was less interested in the value of the piece that he held in his hand than in what it contained. The base was a solid block, and a short inspection revealed its secret. Very carefully he twisted the upper part, holding the lower firmly gripped. After the first initial turn, which was a little difficult, it unscrewed easily.

The interior was hollow. From it he extracted a thin roll of paper. Laying the two halves of the carving aside he carefully unrolled the strip and read the disconnected words which formed the fourth section of the dead man's legacy.

4.
th I
discover
conspir . . .
on J . . .

is plot
power
from a
the pow . . .
use
the c . . .
of any
ey have
ir own
in th . . .
e to
is ru . . .
d save
x men
n Beck,
an Stens . . .
plot a
f these
ater Man . . .
coming
e Britis
se my
taken

Old Aaron watched him curiously, but asked no questions, and when he had come to the end he turned the strip over and glanced at the rhyme on the back. It ran:

'They serve who only stand and wait
Inside the portals of the golden gate.
The head of these, perhaps the best,
Is he you seek, ignore the rest.'

At first glance it appeared to him to be the most difficult of the clues that had so far come into his possession. Folding the slip he put it away in his wallet.

'I will not trouble you any further, Mr. Rosenburg,' he said. 'I am most grateful for your help.'

The old man waved away his thanks. 'I am pleased to have been of assistance,' he said. 'Your country has always treated my people well. If, in however small a way, I can show my gratitude, I am glad to do so.'

Dene gripped the thin hand, and was astonished at the strength with which his clasp was returned.

'If,' continued old Aaron, 'you would mind giving me a receipt for what you have taken . . . '

'Certainly,' said Michael Dene. 'I am sorry, I forgot.'

He scribbled on the sheet of paper which the old Jew pushed towards him and signed his name.

'Thank you,' said Aaron. 'It is just a matter of business, Mr. Dene, and,' he smiled, 'I have the reputation of being good business man.'

He accompanied the Secret Service man to the door and watched him until he was out of sight, then, with a sigh he returned to his desk and the ordinary routine of his business. He had been intensely curious to know what the slip of paper had contained which his visitor had taken from the chess piece, but unless the information had been vouchsafed him freely it was not his place to ask questions.

Dene came out of the pawnshop and crossed the strip of pavement to his waiting car. Colgate-Jones and Peter had remained at the vicarage, at Dene's suggestion, to look after Mary. The Secret Service man was a little troubled concerning the safety of the girl. By now her escape must have been discovered and he was afraid that an effort might be made to recapture her.

Climbing into the driving seat of the big saloon he pressed on the starter and sent the car moving slowly forward, his mind was occupied with a name he had seen among the disjointed words on the slip in his pocket. It was an unfinished name, but it was sufficient to startle him, and taken in conjunction with the previous slip it could only refer to one man — Morgan Stenson, one of the richest men in England, perhaps one of the richest men in the world, and if Jordan had not made a mistake, one of the group whose activities he was trying to circumvent.

Perhaps it was due to his preoccupation that he was less alert than usual. Certainly the first warning he had of danger was the cold ring of steel that pressed into the back of his neck.

'Keep silent and obey my instructions.' whispered a voice in his ear, 'and if you attempt to stop the car or in any way try to attract attention I shall shoot!'

Michael Dene glanced in the mirror in front of him. A man was leaning forward from the back of the car, a man whose broad brimmed hat shadowed his face.

'What do you want?' asked the Secret Service man calmly, although he knew very well the answer to his question.

'I want what you came to that shop to get,' was the answer, 'and I want you! You will drive where I tell you to, unless you prefer a longer and lonelier journey.'

21

Colgate-Jones Becomes Uneasy

It had necessitated a great deal of argument on Michael Dene's part to assure Peter and the clergyman that their presence was unnecessary when he set out on his journey to the pawnshop in Whitechapel. It was only when he pointed out the possible danger to Mary's safety that might accrue from leaving her alone in the vicarage that they capitulated and agreed to remain behind.

Peter, it was true, was not averse to staying with the girl, and it was more the dictates of conscience that prompted him to urge that he should accompany Dene.

Since he had first seen Mary Jordan, on that evening when she had arrived at the vicarage, she had scarcely ever been absent from his thoughts. There was something about her, an illusive quality, which he found difficult to define, that attracted him tremendously. Of a quiet and rather studious disposition, he had, unlike the majority of the men of his age, mixed very little with the opposite sex, and the few he had come in contact with had not impressed him to any great extent. For the most part he considered girls frivolous and shallow and deserving of very little serious attention. But Mary Jordan was different. There was intelligence in her big eyes and she radiated an atmosphere of restfulness. He came to the conclusion that there was no other girl quite like her, and was unaware that this conclusion had been arrived at by thousands of other men before him concerning thousands of other girls, and it was really not Mary Jordan who was different, but the fact that she was different in his eyes.

It was not until late in the afternoon that they began to feel any uneasiness at Dene's non-return. The Secret Service man had stated before leaving that he would come straight back and acquaint them of the result of his visit, but there were a thousand things that might have delayed him, and his continued absence gave them no cause for worry. When, however, it was approaching dinnertime and there was still no sign of Dene, Colgate-Jones put into words the vague fear that had been troubling him for the last hour.

'What can have happened to delay Mr. Dene?' he said, interrupting a low-toned conversation between Peter and the girl. 'He ought to be back by now, surely.'

'Perhaps he's had some other business to attend to,' said Peter. 'Most likely he decided to call in at his office and found something there that held him up.'

The clergyman nodded. 'Perhaps that's it,' he said, 'but I can't help feeling a little worried. He said he'd come straight back.'

'You don't think that anything can — can have happened to him?' asked Mary gravely.

'Well, I don't know,' said Colgate-Jones. 'We've had ample proof that these people are a desperate crew. They've already made one attempt on Dene's life as it is.'

'But they know nothing about the pawnshop,' said Peter.

'No.' The clergyman pursed his lips doubtfully. 'But they may have someone watching him all the same. We were followed to the lock if you remember, and I should think it's pretty certain that we've been watched ever since.'

'Dene is capable of taking care of himself,' said Peter confidently. 'I don't think you've any cause for worry.'

'I hope you're right,' said the vicar. 'But however capable a man is there is such a thing as being taken by surprise. I think I'll ring up his office, anyhow, and see if I can get any news of him.'

He went into the house, returning presently with a serious face.

'He hasn't been there,' he said shortly. 'I don't like it, Clayton. I don't like it at all. It couldn't have taken him all this time to go to Whitechapel and back. He ought to have returned hours ago.'

'Perhaps,' suggested Peter hopefully, although he was beginning to feel as alarmed as the other, 'perhaps he discovered the strip at the pawnshop, found the next clue was an easy one, and is following it up.'

Colgate-Jones agreed that it was a possible suggestion.

'We'll give him a few hours longer,' he said, 'and then I think we ought to do something.'

'What can we do?' asked Peter, and the clergyman shrugged his shoulders.

'I don't know,' he answered candidly. 'But if Michael Dene hasn't returned by bedtime I don't think we ought to sit here doing nothing.'

He relapsed into silence, staring at the slowly flowing river, and Peter and the girl tried to pick up their conversation at the point where he had interrupted them, but their minds were troubled. The possibility that something might have happened to the lean, grey-eyed man whom they had all come to like, threw a gloomy shadow over them and rendered small talk impossible.

Dinner was served and eaten without any sign of the Secret Service man, neither had he put in an appearance when Mrs. Sutherland came to inquire if there was anything more they needed before she retired.

At twelve o'clock, thoroughly alarmed, they packed Mary off to bed, despite her protestations, and sat down to consider the situation.

'Now,' said Colgate-Jones, helping himself to a whisky and soda, 'it seems to me pretty evident that something has happened to Dene, and if that is the case it's up to us. What are we going to do?'

'We can't do anything tonight,' said Peter. 'I think our best course unless we hear something in the meantime, is to go to this pawnshop first thing in the morning and start inquiries from there.'

'That's a pretty sound scheme,' said Colgate-Jones, 'although I doubt if it's going to get us very far. Whatever happened to Dene — if we're not making a mountain out of a molehill — is more likely to have happened after he left the shop.'

Peter nodded gloomily.

'We may be able, however,' he said, 'to trace his movements from there; that car of his is a very conspicuous machine.

Maybe we could find out in which direction he went.'

Colgate-Jones looked none too sanguine.

'The traffic is very thick in Whitechapel,' he said. 'It's doubtful if the car would have been noticed among so many. Didn't you tell me when you first met Dene that he sent over to Scotland Yard for a man called Tilly?'

'Dilly,' corrected Peter. 'Yes, that was the man who arrested me.'

'Well, don't you think,' went on Colgate-Jones, 'that if Dene hasn't returned by the morning the best thing we could do would be to get in touch with Dilly and explain the whole situation? After all, Scotland Yard stand a much more likely chance of tracing the car than we do. They can broadcast its description and cover as much ground in twelve hours as we should in a month.'

Peter was in full agreement with him.

'Why not ring them up now?' he suggested, but Colgate-Jones shook his head.

'I don't want to do anything until we are absolutely sure,' he said. 'There's a possible chance that Dene may have reasons of his own for not returning as he said he would, though I'm inclined to think he would have telephoned. I don't want to go butting in until it's essential.'

Peter gulped the remainder of his drink and lit a cigarette.

'At the same time,' he remarked gravely, 'if he has fallen into the hands of these people, the quicker we do something the better. Delay may mean the difference between life and death.'

'I admit that,' said Colgate-Jones. 'Do you realize, Clayton, that if anything happens to Dene it rests with us to carry on?'

Peter nodded.

'I don't think,' the clergyman continued, 'that he's reported to his office any of his discoveries, and therefore we are the only people who know sufficiently about the matter to put a stop to this conspiracy — whatever it is.'

They continued to discuss the matter until after one, and then, with a suppressed yawn, Colgate-Jones knocked the ashes out of his pipe into the fireplace.

'I don't think it's much good waiting

up any longer,' he remarked. 'If Dene comes now he'll expect to find us in bed and knock us up.'

They were both tired, for nothing is more conducive to weariness than anxiety.

'I'll leave a message for Mrs. Sutherland to call us early,' said the vicar, going over to his desk, and he was in the act of scribbling it when there came a gentle tap at the front door. It sounded plainly in the silence of the sleeping house, and Peter looked at his host.

'There's Dene now,' he said, and there was relief in his voice. 'Shall I go?'

Colgate-Jones nodded, tearing up the partly written message, which he had been going to leave for the housekeeper.

Peter left the study, crossed the dark hall, and opened the front door.

'Hello, Dene!' he began. 'What — '

His startled cry brought Colgate-Jones hastily after him, and the clergyman rapped out an exclamation as be saw the three shadowy figures who had forced their way into the hall.

'Put up your hands!' said a low voice

sharply. 'Waiting for Michael Dene, are you? Well, you'll have to wait a long time. He's not coming back here.'

'What — ?' began Colgate-Jones, but was allowed to go no further.

'Don't talk!' snapped the man who had spoken before. 'You're coming with us, both of you. Go and get the girl!'

Peter felt a wave of rage break over him as one of the men moved towards the staircase.

'You leave her alone!' he cried, 'or I'll — '

'What will you do?' grated the harsh voice, and the muzzle of a pistol ground into his neck. 'What will you do, Mr. Clayton?'

Peter was silent. He realized his utter helplessness to do anything. If he attempted to prevent these men from carrying out their intention he would be shot instantly, and he knew it.

'Tie them up!' said the man, and Colgate-Jones felt his arms seized and jerked behind his back.

He submitted reluctantly, for he was itching to put up a fight for it, but common sense told him that it was useless to attempt to tackle three men, armed men, with bare hands, so he accepted the situation philosophically.

'Take them out to the car,' said the spokesman, when they had both been rendered helpless.

Silent and inwardly raging, they were conducted by an armed guard down the dark drive to where a large closed car was waiting at the gate. Jerking open the door, one of the men with them motioned with the muzzle of his automatic towards the interior.

'Get in!' he whispered.

There was nothing for it but to obey. Their adversaries had won, thought Colgate-Jones bitterly, as he huddled himself into a corner of the padded seat. Dene had already fallen into their hands. And now they had themselves. The only other two people who were a source of danger to the scheme of these crooks, were about to be spirited away and rendered harmless. It was a galling thought, and it sent the blood coursing through his veins angrily.

The man who had led them to the car stood by the open door waiting for his companions. Five minutes passed, and then they put in an appearance accompanied by Mary Jordan. The girl had evidently been forced to dress hurriedly, and as she was pushed into the back of the car with them Peter saw that her hands had been tied behind her in a similar way to their own. One of the men got up behind the driving seat, the other taking his place by his side, and the third man stepped in beside them and closed the door.

'Where are you taking us?' demanded Colgate-Jones as the car moved forward.

'You're going to join your clever friend,' was the reply. 'What will happen to you after that I don't know, but I should think it's doubtful if you'll ever see the world again.'

He spoke quite unemotionally, and Mary uttered a choked, sobbing cry.

'You — you mean,' she whispered huskily, 'that we're going to be killed?'

'I should think nothing was more certain,' said the man coolly.

The girl stared at his dim figure, her eyes wide with terror, and then her over-strained nerves broke. Peter felt her slump sideways against him as a merciful oblivion blotted out sight, sound and thought, and there was despair in his heart as the big car, gathering speed, rushed through the darkness of the night towards its unknown destination.

22

The House on the Moor

At the foot of the Cleveland Hills, facing a wild expanse of open moorland, stands an old house of crumbling grey stone. The grounds which belong to it are weed-grown and neglected, the windows curtainless and dirty; for this place, once the home of a rich Yorkshire family, is now derelict, slowly rotting to destruction.

At first glance it has the appearance of being empty, but the inhabitants of the scattered cottages, which lie in its vicinity, will tell you that this first impression is erroneous. There are stories in the district of a dark, sallow-faced man, with untidy hair, who lives in the Moor House and is occasionally to be seen striding over the bleak and rugged moorland or buying supplies in the neighbouring village of Selkirk, a man who speaks with a foreign accent and is generally supposed to be an eccentric geologist investigating the strata of the Cleveland Hills.

Should anyone with a knowledge of geology have explored the interior of the desolate house they would have been somewhat surprised, for there was nothing in the whole building appertaining to that science.

The largest room on the ground floor had certainly been fitted up as a laboratory, but the tenant's researches into the structure of the earth's crust must have been strange indeed if any of the instruments here were of assistance to his studies.

The room was lit by artificial light produced from a humming dynamo in one corner, for care had been taken to exclude every vestige of daylight. The French windows leading to the garden had been closed and locked and a heavy wooden shutter screwed over them; a smaller window, in the centre of one of the walls, had been treated in a similar manner. Whether it was necessary to the successful carrying out of the work done in this room that no ray of daylight should penetrate was known only to the tenant, but it was more probable that these precautions had been taken with a view to obviating any possibility of an eavesdropper. For in that closely shuttered apartment, on the ground floor of the old house on the edge of the Yorkshire Moors, was the nucleus of the conspiracy that had been hatched against the welfare of Great Britain.

A man was seated at the broad bench that occupied the centre of the laboratory, making careful adjustments to a delicate piece of apparatus. He was completely absorbed in his work, this dark-featured, carelessly dressed man with the high forehead and sallow, unhealthy skin, so absorbed that he failed to hear the knocking on the door, which heralded the arrival of the visitor. When eventually it penetrated to his mind he uttered an impatient exclamation, and rising to his feet went over and turned the key in the lock.

The bald-headed Voles entered, as immaculate as ever, his round, colourless face showing a trace of annoyance.

'I've been knocking for some time, Dostoviski,' he said, a little irritably. 'Didn't you hear me?'

The thin man shook his dishevelled head.

'I heard nothing,' he muttered. 'I was busy.'

Voles glanced round the large room, his eyes flickering over the various pieces of apparatus on the benches.

'You will be ready?' he asked. 'Everything is going well?'

'Everything is going well,' said the other. 'I have improved on the original.'

'Good!' said the bald-headed man. 'Mr. Stenson is coming to see you this evening. He wishes for another demonstration, to make sure.'

'He need have no fear,' said Dostoviski. 'So far as I am concerned everything will be in readiness. I shall need some more quartz and a further supply of the platinum.'

'I will see that you have it,' said Voles. His fat face creased into an ugly smile. 'It will cause a sensation!' he remarked, rubbing his hands. 'A great sensation! We and our friends will be practically masters of the world!'

Dostoviski plunged one of his thin hands into the pockets of his shapeless coat and produced a long Russian cigarette. 'You have come about something else?' he said, when he had lit it. 'Something other than to inform me that Mr. Stenson is coming this evening?'

Voles started. He had experienced this uncanny thought-reading on the part of the other before.

'You are quite right,' he assented. 'I have come to warn you to be prepared to receive guests.'

The sallow-faced man frowned.

'Guests?' he grunted. 'I cannot be bothered with a lot of people; they will interfere with my work. Who are these guests that you talk about?'

'I'll guarantee that they will not interfere with your work.' said Voles. 'I am arranging with Laxton to prepare the cellars for their reception.'

Dostoviski nodded slowly.

'I see,' he murmured. 'These guests you speak of will have no choice but to accept our hospitality. Who are they?'

'The man Dene, two friends of his, and the girl,' answered Voles, and the other raised his eyebrows.

'Why do we bother to keep them prisoners?' he asked. 'Why not — settle with them once and for all?'

'Stenson's orders,' said the bald-headed man briefly. 'I don't know what he's got at the back of his mind.'

'Mr. Stenson is a wonderful man,' said Dostoviski, in his low, soft voice. 'A man of genius. I have great admiration for him. No one who did not possess great intellect could have evolved this scheme on which we are working.'

'He's clever enough,' said Voles. 'Clever as the Devil!'

'I shall be ready to receive him,' said Dostoviski. 'Seven of the instruments are already completed.'

'And you have tested them?' inquired Voles.

The other nodded.

'They work perfectly!' he declared.

The bald-headed man turned to open the door.

'I won't disturb you from your labours any longer,' he said, and when he had gone Dostoviski turned the key behind him and, returning to the bench, became once more absorbed in his work.

23

The Cellar

Michael Dene opened his eyes in utter darkness, and stared vaguely about him. He could see nothing, and in the dazed state that accompanied his return to consciousness was puzzled to account for this blackness and the peculiar musty smell, which appeared to be part and parcel of it.

It was a long time before memory supplied a solution, and then he understood. He remembered coming out of the pawnshop in Whitechapel, getting into his car, and the man who had been concealed in the back.

He had been forced to drive into the open country, the pistol pressing into the small of his back rendering argument useless. He had pulled up at the side of a lonely road and a pad, reeking of some drug, had been pressed over his mouth and nose, and from then until he had wakened in this dark, evil-smelling place, he had known nothing of what had occurred. Whatever the drug was that had been used it had been a pungent one, though curiously enough it had left behind very few unpleasant after effects. His head was a little stuffy and his mouth was a trifle dry, but beyond these symptoms he felt fairly normal.

It was evident that he had been followed from the vicarage to the shop in Whitechapel, and his trailer had taken advantage of the car being empty during his interview with Mr. Rosenburg to conceal himself in the back and take Dene by surprise. It had been so simple, and he cursed himself for having fallen victim to such a childish piece of strategy. But his mind had been so fully occupied with the fresh clue he had picked up at the pawnshop that he had never thought of making sure the car was empty before taking his place at the wheel.

Well, that piece of carelessness was likely to cost him dear, might probably result in his death, for he had no illusions concerning the people into whose hands he had fallen. They were concentrating all their efforts on preventing the secret of this conspiracy, which Jordan had discovered, from becoming known, and he was their greatest danger.

That his wrists and ankles had been tied became evident during a tentative attempt to move, and from the feel of the greasy floor beneath his fingers he concluded that it was stone. This, together with the moist, mildewy odour, suggested something underground, a kind of cellar, or maybe the kitchen where Mary Jordan had been confined. He remembered the girl's description of the place, and, to a certain extent, it tallied.

He had been hoping that when his eyes grew accustomed to the darkness he would be able to see something of his surroundings, but it was so intense that this hope was dispelled.

He wondered whether Colgate-Jones and Peter were worrying over his absence, but since it was impossible for him to tell how long he had been unconscious they might not yet have had any cause. Would they guess what had happened when he failed to put in an appearance? And if so what steps would they take? He had no doubt that they would do something, although the things they could do were limited. Still, Colgate-Jones was no fool. He had great respect for the clergyman's intelligence, almost as great a respect as he had for his fighting ability. A grand man, thought Michael Dene, a man one was proud to number among one's friends.

One of the attributes of his prison was its intense quietness. Although he strained his ears he could hear nothing, not the slightest sound anywhere. It was as still and silent as a tomb.

Immediately the simile occurred to him he decided that it was not a very happy one. This place might very easily prove a tomb indeed. Experience had taught him, however, that it was useless giving way to despair. During the course of his career he had found himself in many predicaments that at first appeared hopeless, and indeed would have been had not his ingenuity discovered a way out. This one might very easily prove similar.

He tested the cords at his wrists and ankles. Whoever had tied him up had been an expert, and he quickly decided that it was useless wasting energy and effort on those. At the present juncture there was nothing he could do except to conserve his strength and try to evolve a means of getting out of this unpleasant position, and even this was useless until he knew more about his surroundings.

His thoughts turned to Jordan's last clue, the rhyme on the back of the slip he had taken from the ivory carving in the pawnshop. He remembered how it went and silently repeated it:

'They serve who only stand and wait
Inside the portals of the golden gate.
The head of these, perhaps the best,
Is he you seek, ignore the rest.'

On the face of it, it seemed very difficult, but it would at least serve to occupy his mind, and in the event of his being able to escape would save time if he could find a solution.

'They serve who only stand and wait.' That was a quotation from somewhere, or almost a quotation. He couldn't remember from where, or exactly how the real quotation ran, but he was under the impression that Jordan's version was not correct. Evidently he had twisted it to suit his purpose. The question was, what was the purpose?

'Inside the portals of the golden gate.' The most usual definition of the 'golden gate' was the entrance to Heaven, but it seemed hardly likely that this was the location of Jordan's fifth strip. It occurred to him grimly that if it was he stood a very good chance, in the circumstances, of finding it. No, the 'golden gate' in this instance must refer to something more material, a place or a building perhaps. But what place or building was likely to possess such an extraordinary name?

For half an hour he pondered, going over in his mind every possible place the name might denote, but without result. He was on the point of giving it up and turning his attention to the last two lines when a simple suggestion offered itself

— a nightclub! A nightclub or one of the lesser-known restaurants with which London abounds.

He considered the suggestion. The more he considered it, the more certain he became that he had found Jordan's meaning. Taking the fact that the 'Golden Gate' was the name of a restaurant or club, what effect did this have on the rest of the rhyme? Who were they who served by standing and waiting? — and the answer to this was immediate — the waiters. Provided the Golden Gate referred to the type of place, he believed it was obvious, and the rest of the verse fitted perfectly. 'The head of these, perhaps the best, is he you seek, ignore the rest,' must refer to the headwaiter.

So the man to whom Jordan had sent the fifth section of the record of his discovery was the headwaiter at a place called the 'Golden Gate'.

Michael Dene was elated at his successful elucidation. It was true that it entirely depended on the fact that his definition of the words 'Golden Gate' was the right one, but since everything else dropped into the right place so smoothly, he was pretty certain that this was so. Confirmation anyhow, would not be difficult once he was in the position to follow up the clue, and that brought his mind back to his present situation

The mental exercise involved in working out the meaning of the rhyme had clarified his brain, and he began to think of possible schemes for escape. It occurred to him, reasonably enough, that if the people into whose hands he had fallen intended killing him they would have done so immediately. There seemed no point in bringing him to this place, wherever it was, unless the intention was to keep him prisoner. Far less risk, from their point of view, would have been involved if they had shot him in the car and left his body to be discovered at the side the lonely road where his captor had forced him to draw up. Since they had gone to the trouble of making him prisoner, it seemed only sensible to suppose that for the present at any rate he was not in danger of losing his life.

Just why this reprieve had been granted

he was unable to conjecture. Maybe the reason lay in his position as head of the special Branch. It was quite possible that the group who had conceived this plot, which Jordan had unearthed, were chary of raising the hue and cry that would result from his murder. More likely they were undecided in their own minds whether he had taken anyone in his department into his confidence. Whatever the reason was, however, the fact remained that had they been going to kill him they would have killed him before now, and the realization was a ray of comfort. Where there's life there's hope is a very trite and moth-eaten phrase, but like most trite and moth-eaten phrases a very true one.

A sound interrupted his musing, a faint thud that seemed to come from somewhere above. He listened intently, but at first he could hear nothing further, then, almost undistinguishable, he heard footsteps.

They became clearer as they drew nearer. There was the dull clank of metal, the grinding rasp of a rusty hinge, and a soft click. A light sprang up above his head, dazzling him after that intense darkness and causing him to blink painfully. It came from a bulkhead light screwed into one of the heavy wooden rafters which he saw supported the ceiling of the place in which he lay.

It was a low-roofed, long apartment, the walls and floor of stone, and in one corner of which was an iron door — a cellar of sorts.

Michael Dene had no time to take in all the details although there were not many. The place was devoid of furniture. His interest was centred on the man who stood in the now open doorway.

He recognized him instantly from Mary's description. There was the bald head and unhealthy-coloured face; the small crimson mouth and the cold blue eyes, and his voice when he spoke held the lisping quality which the girl had so vividly described.

'So you have recovered consciousness, Mr. Dene,' he said, advancing and picking his way delicately over the dirty flooring. 'I trust that you feel no unpleasant effects from the drug that was administered to you?'

The Secret Service man looked up at him steadily.

'You have the advantage of me,' he said coolly. 'Who are you?'

'It is unnecessary that you should know my name,' said Voles. 'But when you say that I have the advantage of you, you speak the truth. I regret that it was necessary to bring you here, and I am afraid that you will find your sojourn a trifle uncomfortable. But you were beginning to make yourself a nuisance to quite a number of people, and we were forced to put a stop to it.'

'At the orders of Mr. Morgan Stenson, I presume?' said Dene curtly, and the bald-headed man's eyes narrowed.

'You know a great deal more than is good for you,' he said. 'I presume you learned that from the very indiscreet document which our poor friend, Norris Jordan, went to so much trouble to concoct?'

'Does it matter how I became aware of it?' asked the Secret Service man.

'Not in the least,' said Voles, shaking his head. 'But I doubt if you could have discovered it from any other source. We have the portions of Jordan's report which you have already succeeded in tracing in our possession; we found them in a wallet in your breast pocket, so I naturally concluded that that is where you gained your knowledge.' He ran plump fingers round his smooth hairless chin.

Michael Dene said nothing. He began to understand something of the terror which this man had inspired in Mary Jordan. There was something completely inhuman about him.

'It has been my misfortune, Mr. Dene,' the stout man continued, and there was a sneer in his voice, 'that I have not met you before. I am told that you are a man of intelligence, and therefore a rarity. Your career in charge of the British Secret Service has, no doubt, been an exciting one. I trust that its termination will not prove an anti-climax.'

'You appear to be under the erroneous impression that I am resigning!' retorted Dene. 'I assure you that there is no question of my career terminating at present.'

The small crimson mouth of the man standing over him curled into an unpleasant smile.

'It seems that you also have erroneous ideas,' he remarked. 'You may not be resigning, Mr. Dene, but your career will terminate, just the same, after the twenty-seventh of next month.'

So, thought Dene, that was the date fixed for his death. For some reason or other these people were going to defer killing him until after the conspiracy reached its culminating point.

'A lot may happen between now and then,' he said steadily.

Voles inclined his head.

'A lot will happen,' he answered. 'By then, Mr. Dene, an upheaval will have taken place in the present era of civilization. The face of the world will be altered, the old traditions will crumble, the old standards will be destroyed.' He stopped abruptly, as though realizing that he was saying too much.

'You are confident,' said Dene. 'But

there is such a thing as over-confidence. One man has already discovered your secret, and what one can do another can do.'

'You were our only danger!' retorted the bald-headed man, 'and you are a danger no longer.'

'There are others,' said Michael Dene, 'who know as much as I.'

'We are aware of that,' said Voles, 'but they are unlikely to interfere with our plans. It occurred to us that during your enforced stay as our guest you might possibly feel a little lonely. We therefore took steps to ensure that you should have congenial company.'

With his quick, mincing walk he went over to the open doorway.

'Bring the others in!' he ordered, and Dene's heart sank as he guessed what the order portended. 'There is no need for me to introduce either the gentlemen or the lady,' said Voles, mouthing the words with relish. 'They are old friends of yours Mr. Dene, and you should be grateful to us for our consideration.'

Michael Dene said nothing, and his

face was expressionless as Colgate-Jones, Peter, and Mary Jordan, securely bound, were carried in and laid on the stone flagged floor of that uncomfortable prison-house.

24

The Swinging Stone

'I've no doubt,' said the bald-headed man, 'that you and your friends would prefer to be alone. Food will be brought to you later, and until then you can rest assured of strict privacy.'

He signalled to the men who had brought Peter, Colgate-Jones and the girl, and when they had departed made his own exit, closing and barring the heavy door behind him.

'So they got you, too,' said Dene, twisting on his side so that he faced his companions in misfortune.

'They did!' growled Colgate-Jones ruefully, 'and we seem to be in a devil of a mess.'

'I'm afraid we are,' agreed the Secret Service man. 'We have, however, one small thing to be thankful for, and that is that they've left the light on. This is hardly what you would call a comfortable place, but it's infinitely worse in the dark.'

'How did they get hold of you?' asked Peter, and Dene told him briefly.

'H'm!' commented Colgate-Jones. 'They weren't so subtle over us.' He related what had happened at the vicarage.

'What do you think they are going to do with us, Mr. Dene?' asked Mary. Her face was white and frightened, but her voice was steady enough.

'From what the unpleasant-looking man said just now,' replied Dene, 'I don't think we've anything to fear until the twenty-seventh of next month.'

'Well, that's something to be thankful for,' growled the clergyman. 'What happens after that?'

'We fade out!' said Dene simply.

'You mean they'll kill us then?' said the girl, and he nodded.

'I'm afraid so,' he said. 'But that's a long time ahead. Anything may happen before then.'

'Why the delay?' inquired Peter. 'Why don't they finish the job at once?'

'That's been puzzling me,' said the

Secret Service man, 'and I can only conclude that for some reason or other they are under the impression that we shall be more use to them alive than dead.'

Colgate-Jones sighed.

'Well, it looks very much to me,' he said, 'as though they've won. I must say I'd like to have had a longer run for my money.

'We're not finished yet,' said Michael Dene.

'Pretty nearly,' grunted Peter. 'There doesn't look much chance of getting out of this place.' He looked round the damp, forbidding stone walls. 'Even if we were free to move about, we shouldn't be much better off. The door is made of solid iron, and the walls and floor look as if they're a foot thick!'

'Talking of being free,' said Colgate-Jones, 'suppose we try to see what we can do in that respect. It may not help us a lot, but I'd infinitely rather be on my feet than lie on this confoundedly damp floor.'

'I've tried,' replied Dene, 'and so far as I'm concerned there's nothing doing, but perhaps they were more careless in tying you three up, so go ahead.'

He watched while the three of them made desperate efforts to loosen their bonds.

'I'm afraid it's hopeless,' gasped Colgate-Jones at last, his face scarlet with exertion. 'The late, lamented Houdini couldn't extricate himself if he'd ever been tied up like this!'

'Same here,' growled Peter. 'The man who trussed me up knew his job.'

'I think,' said Mary, 'that I might be able to get my hands free. I don't know whether they took less trouble with me, but I seem to have succeeded in loosening the cords at my wrists.'

'Have you?' said Dene quickly. 'That's fine! If you can manage to get free, Miss Jordan, you can release us!'

'Be careful!' warned Peter. 'That fellow said something about bringing us food. If he does, and finds we've succeeded in getting loose, he'll only tie us up again, and we shall have had all our trouble for nothing.'

'There's something in that!' agreed the

Secret Service man. 'Anyhow, there's no harm in Miss Jordan seeing what she can do.'

The girl strained and tugged, forcing her wrists apart, and after a little while there was no longer any doubt that the cords were giving. Each successive effort reduced their tightness.

'I think I can pull my hands through now,' she informed them, panting.

'Well, don't at the moment,' said Dene. 'Wait, as Peter suggests, until after we are sure of not being disturbed.'

The warning was timely, for he had barely uttered it when they heard the sound of approaching footsteps. The iron bar securing the door fell with a clang; the key grated in the lock; and it opened to admit a surly-faced man who carried a large plate of sandwiches and a jug of coffee.

''Ere's yer supper,' he growled, and they were the only words he spoke during the time he remained in the cellar.

'Now,' whispered Dene, looking across at Mary, 'if you can free your hands, I don't think we are likely to be disturbed again for some time.'

The girl nodded, and once more she strained at the cords. It was difficult, but slowly and painfully she succeeded in pulling one of her hands out from the encircling rope. Her skin was raw and chafed in the process, but she cared little for that in the pleasure of her success.

'I've done it!' she said, sitting up and, leaning forward, she began to pick at the knots that secured her ankles. A second later she was free and rose unsteadily to her feet.

Dene noticed that she went to Peter first, and suppressed a smile. When he had been released he came over to the Secret Service man and set about untying him while Mary did the same to Colgate-Jones. It was a relief to stretch their cramped limbs, and they occupied their first few moments of freedom by rubbing their wrists and ankles vigorously to restore the circulation.

'That's better,' said Dene, getting to his feet. 'The next step is to find a way out of this prison.'

'And that,' remarked Colgate-Jones, 'is

not going to be easy.'

He began to search his pockets quickly, and uttered an exclamation of satisfaction when he brought to light a cigarette case and lighter.

'I was afraid they might have taken them,' he said, holding the case out to Dene and Peter. 'A smoke, when there's a problem to face, makes all the difference in the world.'

'I'd like one, too,' said Mary, and with a muttered apology he passed the case over to her.

Dene inhaled the smoke gratefully and began an examination of the cellar. It did not take him long to realize that their chances of getting out were very remote. The door was impassable, the hinges were sunk in the solid concrete, and it fitted closely into a concrete surround. Neither did the walls look any more promising. They were built of large blocks of grey stone cemented together and covered with the grime and slime of years. The flooring was similar, and there was no window. He looked up at the ceiling, which was composed of heavy beams supporting a solid floor. There was no sign of a trap or any means of entrance or exit other than the door.

'Well,' remarked Peter, 'it's something to be able to move about, though I think that's as far as we can get.'

'It certainly looks like it,' agreed the Secret Service man. 'Nothing short of a dynamite charge would shift that door, and the same thing applies to the walls.'

'I suppose,' said Colgate-Jones, 'they won't bring us any more food until tomorrow morning?'

'I shouldn't think so,' said Dene. 'Are you feeling hungry?'

'I am,' said the clergyman, 'but I wasn't thinking of that. It occurred to me that if that stolid-faced fellow comes again it shouldn't be difficult for the three of us to take him by surprise.'

'The same idea has occurred to me,' said Dene. 'There's certainly a chance there. I believe it's a scheme that might be successful.'

The possibility of escape had produced a more cheerful feeling among them.

'I wish they'd left us some form of

warmth,' said Peter, stamping his feet. 'It may be summer outside, but it's like December down here.'

There was some truth in what he said. The cold, damp air of the cellar struck chill to their bones, and the prospect of spending a night in that atmosphere was not pleasant.

'It isn't altogether warm,' said Colgate-Jones, 'but we can't expect everything.' He followed Peter's example and began to stamp his feet.

'We shall have — ' began Dene, and stopped as the clergyman uttered an exclamation. 'What is it?' he asked.

'It sounds hollow here,' said Colgate-Jones excitedly. 'Listen!'

He stamped again, and then moving to another part of the floor repeated the process. The sound was certainly different, and Dene came hurriedly to his side. At the spot where Colgate-Jones had been standing he beat a tattoo with one foot, and, as the vicar had said, there was a distinctly hollow sound. Going down on his knees, the Secret Service man peered closely at the floor.

The interstices between the stones were so encrusted with dirt that at first he could see nothing unusual in that particular portion. With the aid of a key which Peter found in his pocket, however, he began methodically to scrape the muck away from the joins, and presently laid bare a square flagstone, which was not embedded in cement like the others.

Holding on to Peter's shoulder for support, he jumped heavily on one side of the stone, but it remained immovable. He repeated the process on the other side with a like result, and then, as he came to the third side he felt a slight movement under his feet.

'Give me a hand here,' he muttered, and getting down on his knees pressed at the point that had given. The stone dropped an eighth of an inch. Colgate-Jones and Peter added their weight, and with a grating sound the big slab swung downward on a central pivot to expose a narrow opening and the beginning of a flight of steps.

'The most wonderful thing about miracles is that they sometimes happen,' quoted Michael Dene, peering down into the darkness. 'Come on, let's explore and see where it goes to.'

'You'd better stay here, Mary,' suggested Colgate-Jones, as Dene swung himself through the opening and began to descend the steps. 'We don't know what may be down there.'

'Whatever there is,' said the girl, 'I'm coming, too. I'm not going to be left here.'

'It seems all right,' called Dene. 'The air's breathable, anyway.'

The steps led down into the bowels of the earth, and there was a stale, unhealthy smell. The Secret Service man counted fifteen and found himself standing at the entrance to a narrow passage with a brick arch. The others joined him, and with the aid of Colgate-Jones' lighter Dene led the way along the tunnel. It did not extend very far, fifty yards at the most, he calculated and then they came upon another flight of steps leading upwards. Mounting these he saw in the dim flame of the lighter, that they ended under a stone similar to the one in the cellar they had just left. It was possible to see the rusty iron pivot on which it swung. Giving the light to Peter to hold, Dene put up his hands and pressed on one end. It remained as solid as a rock.

Having come so far, it was going to prove disappointing if they could not find a means of exit. He ascended two steps higher, crouched, and getting his shoulders firmly against the stone trap, strained upwards with all his strength. Three times he tried without success, but at the fourth attempt, with a rasping grunt, the stone gave slightly.

Peter came to his assistance, and between them they forced the heavy slab upwards. It was a similar contrivance to the other, pivoted in the centre so that half swung up and half swung down,

'Now let's see where we've got to,' said Dene, and emerged into darkness.

Bending down he took the light, which Peter held up to him, and as the others climbed through the open trap looked about him.

He discovered that the passage admitted them to a cellar, which was almost an exact counterpart of the one they had left except that it was larger and stacked from floor to roof with square wooden boxes. There were hundreds of these, ranged in orderly array round the walls.

'What are they?' grunted Colgate-Jones, staring at them, but Dene shook his head. 'Stores I should think,' he replied. 'Lucky for us they weren't stacked on the top of the trap, otherwise it would have been impossible to open it.'

'I don't know that we're any better off,' said Peter, 'now that we've got here. Is that door closed like the other one? If it is we're jiggered!'

Michael Dene went over and tried it.

'I'm afraid we're jiggered,' he said, and there was no sign of the disappointment he felt in his voice. 'We've merely got out of one cellar into another.'

'Well it can't be helped,' remarked the clergyman as cheerfully as he could. 'I'd like to know what's in these boxes. If it's stores, as you suggest, they've got enough for a regiment.' He stooped and tried to lift one of the crates, uttering an exclamation of surprise as he found that it was impossible to move it. 'Good Heavens!' he gasped, 'What can the thing contain? You try and shift it, Dene. It's like trying to move a solid lump of lead.'

The Secret Service man tried.

'It's curious,' he remarked, frowning. 'It can't contain stores at any rate. There's nothing in the eating line that would weigh as heavily as this. I'd like to open one of these boxes,'

Peter, who had been roaming about with Mary, picked up a steel claw.

'This'll do the trick,' he said, holding it out.

The Secret Service man took it. Inserting the claw under one of the planks that formed the top of the box he had tried to shift, he levered it up. It came with a protesting squeak and, wrenching it off, he peered at the contents.

'Looks like a solid block of lead,' he said at once, and pressed with his finger at the dull metallic surface, which had been exposed.

'No, it isn't solid,' he exclaimed. 'It's only lead foil! Let's see what there is beneath.'

With the point of the crowbar he

ripped the covering open, and enlarging the hole with his hands, uttered an exclamation of astonishment as he saw what it had concealed.

Packed closely together was a row of yellow bars. With difficulty he lifted one out.

'Gold!' he muttered aghast, and the others stared at him, amazement in their eyes.

'Gold!' breathed Colgate-Jones. 'It can't be, Dene!'

'It is,' said the Secret Service man. 'Feel the weight of this.' He passed the ingot to the clergyman, and it was all Colgate-Jones could do to hold it.

'And there are hundreds of similar cases!' said Peter. 'If they all contain gold this place must hold a fortune.'

Michael Dene nodded. The discovery of this treasure house had amazed him, and he was wondering what part this hidden store of gold was to play in the conspiracy which Norris Jordan had unearthed; the conspiracy which aimed at the downfall of Great Britain. And of the details of which, up till now, he knew nothing.

25

When the Lights Went Out

Mr. Morgan Stenson, his small body huddled among the cushions of his luxurious car, stared through the window at the dark countryside as the huge machine ran smoothly through the night. A cigar was clenched between his teeth, but it had long since gone out, testifying to the concentration of his thoughts.

The colossal plan, which his astute brain had conceived, and on which he had spent the greater part of fifteen years perfecting, was nearing completion. He had overcome obstacle after obstacle, and the last of these, the possible danger of Michael Dene's interference, had given him a great deal of worry. That was over now.

The car turned off the main road, negotiated a secondary feeder, and cane out on to the bleak, open moorland. Mr.

Stenson leaned forward, switched on the light for a moment, and glanced at his watch. Twenty minutes to twelve! He would reach his destination at the time he had said, and the knowledge gave him satisfaction. One of his main characteristics was his mania for punctuality; it amounted almost to a fetish. If he made an appointment he liked to arrive at exactly the time stipulated, neither before nor after.

Plunging the inside of the car in darkness once more, he leaned back and allowed his mind to dwell on the future. If the scheme succeeded he and the group of men with him would be all-powerful!

The knowledge thrilled him as very few things were able to these days, for during his life he had acquired everything that he wanted and was satiated in consequence. The only thing now that stirred his thin blood was power, and unlimited power would shortly be his.

His thoughts were very pleasant as the car turned through the crumbling stone gateway that gave admittance to the winding drive of Moor House. It had been an accident that had led him to discover this place, so ideally suited to his needs. Motoring through the district, the car had broken down near the village of Selkirk. While it was being repaired he had taken a walk on the moor and had come upon the house in all its desolation. A week later he had bought it, through one of his agents. There was nothing to connect Mr. Morgan Stenson himself with the transaction, and the most stringent inquiry would have failed to reveal that the purchase money had come out of his pocket.

This had happened ten years ago, when the great scheme, which had its genesis in the dying words of a crazy Polish scientist, was in an embryonic state.

The car came to a halt before the moss-covered steps; the chauffeur alighted and held open the door while Mr. Stenson got nimbly out. So far as outward appearance went, the house might have been deserted; no glimmer of light broke the blackness of its forbidding exterior. The door, however, opened immediately in answer to the chauffeur's soft knock, and as they entered the dimly lit hall Voles came forward to greet his employer.

'Punctual as usual, sir,' he remarked.

Stenson nodded curtly.

'See that Mason is looked after, will you?' he said, jerking his head towards the chauffeur. 'He's had a long drive and will probably be in need of a meal.'

Voles signalled to the man who had opened the door.

'Take Mr. Stenson's chauffeur along to the kitchen.' he ordered. 'See that he has everything he wants.'

The man departed, accompanied by the chauffeur, and Voles turned to Stenson.

'If there is anything you would like?' he inquired. 'A glass of wine, or a whisky and soda — '

'No, I want nothing.' said Stenson, shaking his head. 'Has Dostoviski got everything ready?'

'I haven't seen him since this afternoon,' said Voles. 'He's locked himself up in the laboratory and won't admit anyone.'

'Tell him I'm here,' said Stenson, 'and

ask him how long it will be before I can witness the demonstration.'

He turned abruptly away and entered a small room on the right of the hall that was shabbily furnished as a lounge. Dropping into an easy chair he took a cigar from his pocket, bit off the end, and lighted it. For some seconds he smoked evenly, waiting the return of Voles. When he came in Stenson looked at him inquiringly.

'Dostoviski says he'll be ready in half an hour,' he announced.

Stenson grunted.

'That'll do,' he said. 'I want to leave here by two at the latest. You've got the man Dene and the others here?'

Voles nodded.

'Yes,' he replied. 'As I told you on the telephone, everything went off without a hitch.'

'Good!' said Stenson.

'Do you want to see them?' asked Voles.

The other shook his head.

'No,' he answered shortly. 'Why should I want to see them? All I want is to be assured that they are safe and can do no further mischief.'

'They're safe enough,' said Voles.

'It is necessary,' continued Stenson, 'that you find out from Dene whether he has divulged what he knows to anyone else. I don't mind what means you use to acquire the information,' — he looked meaningfully at the other — 'but it is essential that we should find that out. If he has spoken of his discovery to anyone else, steps must be taken to make certain that that person cannot send on his knowledge, you understand?'

'I understand perfectly,' said Voles. 'Dene is aware that you are connected with this business.'

Stenson rapped out an oath.

'How did you become aware of that?' he asked.

'Your name was mentioned in the portion of Jordan's document, which he had already succeeded in gaining possession of,' answered the bald-headed man.

Putting his hand in his pocket be took out Michael Dene's wallet and exhibited the strips, Stenson peered at them, frowning.

'Jordan was cleverer than I imagined,' he said. 'He found out a great deal more than I expected.' He read the clue on the back of the last strip and looked up. 'This must be followed up!' he snapped. 'The remainder of this precious document must be discovered at all costs.' He handed the slips of paper back to Voles. 'Bring that rhyme to me tomorrow afternoon,' he said, 'and I'll work out the solution.'

'What shall I do with these?' said Voles. 'Destroy them?'

Stenson shook his head.

'No, you'd better keep them for the moment,' he said. 'I should like to see the thing in its entirety.' He drew deeply at his cigar and sent a cone of smoke ceiling-wards from between his thin lips. 'There will be another consignment of gold on Saturday,' he announced abruptly. 'You will notify Denham to expect it.'

'Will that be the last?' inquired Voles.

'No,' answered Stenson, 'there'll be another on the twenty-second, that will be the last. These men you have employed to guard the place, they are unaware of the contents of the boxes?'

'Yes,' answered the bald-headed man. 'They are under the impression that they contain ammunition.'

An unpleasant, smile flickered for an instant over the wizened face of his employer.

'Not altogether a wrong definition,' he murmured. 'Gold is the finest ammunition in the world, Voles. It's just as well they are ignorant, though, I don't trust any of these rabble! Dostoviski knows, of course — '

'Dostoviski knows,' said Voles, 'but he's not interested in anything except his science. Gold to him is in the same category as iron, steel or any other metal — a substance which reacts to certain chemicals.'

He looked round as the door opened and Dostoviski intruded his dishevelled head.

'I'm ready now,' he said.

Stenson rose.

'Are you satisfied?' he inquired.

The Russian nodded.

'More than satisfied,' he answered. 'I

have improved on the original idea out of all knowledge. Come and judge for yourself.'

He led the way across the hall to the door of the laboratory. Ushering them in, he closed it behind him and walked over to the central bench on which stood a complicated piece of apparatus, in size and appearance not unlike a portable wireless set, except that where the loudspeaker would have been was a squat, trumpet-shaped reflector of quartz.

'This has a range of half a mile,' he said, touching the apparatus lovingly with his stained fingers, 'and will penetrate any substance with the exception of quartz.'

He jerked his head towards a row of boxes that were scattered on one of the benches that ran round the wall. There were concrete boxes, wooden boxes, steel boxes, iron boxes, boxes constructed from every conceivable substance, including glass.

'You have experimented on all those?' asked Stenson.

Dostoviski nodded.

'Yes, and with success,' he replied.

The small eyes of the multi-millionaire glistened.

'Show me!' he demanded curtly.

'I must have more gold,' said the Russian. 'I have used up my supply.'

'I'll fetch some,' said Voles. 'How much do you want?'

'An ingot will do.'

The bald man left the laboratory, and while he was gone the Russian answered several questions put to him by Stenson concerning the apparatus on the bench. It is doubtful if his replies contributed a great deal to Stenson's knowledge, for they were couched in a technical language which was beyond him. If it was so he made no parade of his ignorance but nodded wisely as he listened to the scientist's staccato sentences. There was an enormous streak of vanity in Morgan Stenson, which prohibited him admitting that he failed to understand anything.

'Voles is a long time,' he said suddenly, becoming aware of the bald-headed man's continued absence, as Dostoviski ceased speaking.

'Perhaps he requires assistance,' said

the Russian. 'He may be having difficulty in opening one of the boxes. Shall I go and see?'

Stenson nodded, and the other crossed to the door. His hand was outstretched to grasp the handle when, without warning, all the lights went out, plunging the room into utter darkness.

26

The Get-Away

Michael Dene stood frowning in silence, staring at the orderly array of boxes, which represented riches almost incalculable. The finding of this hidden store of gold had astonished him considerably.

'What can they want it for?' muttered Colgate-Jones. 'They must have been amassing it for years.'

The Secret Service man nodded. He could offer no suggestion beyond the obvious one that it was to be used for the expenses of the conspiracy, which he was trying to discover and circumvent. But this seemed an inadequate explanation. If it was merely to be used to finance the plot, notes would have been of equal value and both easier to obtain and easier to store. The acquiring of so much gold must have been a difficult business. At a rough calculation he estimated that there must be almost the equivalent here as represented the entire gold reserve of the country. The purchase value must have run into millions, and although he was aware that the group which he was up against constituted the richest men in the world, he concluded that it must have tried even their resources to have found sufficient capital to buy this colossal amount of bullion.

An examination of the gold cellar showed that there was as little hope of escape from that as from the other.

'We don't seem to be much better off,' remarked Peter, and Colgate-Jones and Dene had to agree with him.

'What do we do now?' said the clergyman.

'I think our best proceeding,' answered Michael Dene, 'is to go back through the passage to the other cellar and try to overcome the man when he brings us our next supply of food. There's no possible hope, so far as I can see, of getting out any other way.'

They were on the point of putting his suggestion into practice when Mary caught Peter by the arm.

'Listen!' she whispered. 'There's somebody coming!'

Dene snapped out the feeble glimmer of the lighter.

'She's right!' he breathed, as he heard the faint sound of approaching footsteps. 'Maybe it's our chance! Get over by the door and be prepared to tackle anyone who comes in.'

They tiptoed over and took up their positions by the iron door, and they had barely done so when a light in the roof came on suddenly, flooding the place with light. Like the one to the other cellar, it was obviously operated from a switch outside the door. The clink of metal followed and a clang as the bar dropped, then came the scrape of a key in the lock and the door was pulled slowly open.

Holding their breath, they crouched in the shelter provided by the opening door and waited for the newcomer to put in an appearance. It was the bald-headed man who entered. He advanced with his mincing steps towards the boxes, and as he turned Dene sprang at him.

He saw the astonishment in the man's eyes, saw the small crimson mouth open, and covered it with his hand before the cry that rose in Voles' throat could be uttered. At the same time Colgate-Jones pinioned his arms and Peter gripped his ankles. A quick jerk brought him down.

'Quick!' said Dene to Mary, as he stifled the struggling man's cries. 'Slip along to the other cellar and get those cords.'

She nodded and hurried away.

Voles fought like a tiger but his strength was no match for the three of them, and by the time the girl had returned Dene had forced his handkerchief into the man's mouth and tied it in place with Peter's. Turning him over on his face, they bound his wrists tightly behind his back and did the same to his ankles. In a few seconds he was lying trussed up and helpless, staring at them with pale eyes full of hatred.

'That's that!' said Dene, a little breathless from his exertions. 'Now, if we can manage to dodge the other inhabitants of this place we stand a pretty good chance of getting away.'

He went over to the door and peered out. Beyond was a stone passage with a flight of steps heading upwards into the darkness. With a word to his companions to wait, he mounted these cautiously and discovered that they led to an open door of heavy oak that gave admittance to the house above. Pausing on the threshold of this he listened intently, but could hear nothing.

Coming back, halfway down the stairs he beckoned to Colgate-Jones, Peter and the girl.

'Come on,' he whispered. 'There doesn't seem to be anyone about.'

They followed him, and emerging through the door, found themselves in darkness. After listening again, Dene produced the lighter, and in the feeble glimmer of the little wick they saw that they were standing in a large, old-fashioned kitchen. A door at one end was closed, but before exploring further Dene decided that it would be wise if they armed themselves with some kind of weapon in case the rest of the household should take them by surprise.

Mentioning this to Peter, they left Colgate-Jones with the girl while they returned to the gold cellar. Peter picked up the crow-bar while Dene stooped over the bound figure of Voles and made a rapid search of his pockets. The first thing he brought to light was his own wallet. A glance inside assured him that the contents were still intact and he thrust it into his pocket, continuing to look for the weapon which he hoped the other might have been carrying. He found it in the hip pocket of the bald man's immaculate trousers, a small but useful automatic. There was a fresh clip of cartridges in the butt and he gave a grunt of satisfaction.

'Come on,' he said to Peter. 'The fates have been kind to us. With any luck we ought to get out of this mess.'

They followed him back to the kitchen, and as they entered the little lighter, which had done so much service, went out, leaving nothing but a red spark of wick.

Michael Dene stopped, suppressing an exclamation of annoyance. It was a nuisance that the petrol had chosen that particular moment for giving out. He had no idea of the lay of the land, and it was worse than useless to fumble about in the dark; to do so was asking for trouble, for they might easily stumble over something and so attract the attention of their enemies.

'Keep still!' he whispered, and moved stealthily over to the door by which they had entered. Closing it softly, he felt about on the way, and presently discovered, as he had hoped, an electric light switch. Pressing it down he put on a light, an un-shaded bulb that hung from a flex over the table. It was a risk, but was a risk that had to be taken.

Glancing swiftly about, he saw another door near the open one, which led down to the cellars. It was ajar, and going over he looked to see what lay beyond. As he had half expected it opened on to a scullery containing another, heavier door, which obviously led into the open. Rather to his surprise, it was neither locked nor bolted, and opening it he peered out into the darkness of the garden. The warm scent of the summer night came to his nostrils, a pleasant smell after the fetid atmosphere of the cellars, and he listened. He could hear nothing.

Beckoning to the others he was in the act of crossing the threshold to freedom when a thought struck him. When he had put on the light in the kitchen he had noticed above the door, near the switch, a fuse-box. It occurred to him that if all the lights in the house were put out, it would render possible pursuit more difficult.

He tiptoed back, found a chair by the table, placed it against the wall and, cautiously mounting, swiftly withdrew the fuses one by one. The light in the kitchen went out as he pulled the last one from the socket, and stepping hurriedly from the chair he ran back to the other three.

'Come on,' he said. 'Let's go while the going's good!'

They hurried out into the garden. Michael Dene, who was the last, slipped the key from the inside of the door, closed it behind him and locked it, flinging the key away into a clump of bushes. A narrow path led from the back door through a tangled mass of shrubbery, and they followed it. It curved sharply to the left, and rounding the bend they came face to face with a man.

'Hello!' exclaimed a gruff voice. 'Who — '

The words ended in a choked cry as Dene's fist shot out and caught the speaker on the point of the jaw. He staggered backwards, and before he could recover the Secret Service man gripped Mary by the arm.

'Run!' he hissed between his teeth, and they flew down the rest of the path like the wind, but the alarm had been given.

Even as they came out on to a broad expanse of rank grass they heard some shouting behind them and from various points in the darkness came answering calls. Dene paused for a moment, his mind working rapidly. From the location of these voices, he guessed what he ought to have expected, that the grounds were patrolled, and unless they were careful they might quite easily run into another of the guards.

'This way,' he said, after a second.

'Keep close to me.'

He set off across a neglected lawn towards a belt of trees that showed dimly in the darkness. They were halfway across when a chorus of shouts warned them that they had been seen. Somewhere behind a shot rang out, and the whine of a bullet came clearly to Dene's ears as it whistled over their heads.

'Put every ounce into it!' he said. 'If we can reach those trees we are comparatively safe.'

A second shot followed immediately on his words, and then a third, a fourth. The sound of running footsteps came to them as they reached the end of the grass patch and began to scramble up a weed-covered bank.

At the top was a broken wooden fence. Trusting to luck what lay on the other side, the Secret Service man vaulted this and turned to assist Mary. The girl almost fell into his arms, and when he had assured himself that Colgate-Jones and Peter had surmounted the obstacle, he continued on his way up the incline that was studded thickly with trees.

There was no more shooting; he concluded that the pursuers had realized the futility of firing at an unseen target and was thankful.

It was difficult going up the hillside, and by the time they reached the crest Mary was almost spent

'Stick at it,' whispered Dene encouragingly. 'It'll be easier now.'

Without the slightest idea where it might lead, Dene turned to the right. The narrow lane — it was little more — continued for some distance and then broadened. Presently he espied a solitary cottage, and was passing it without a second glance when he saw something that caused him to pull up abruptly, to the surprise of his companions.

'What is it?' asked Colgate-Jones. 'What are you stopping for?'

For answer Dene pointed to the vague outline of a car that stood in a small enclosure by the side of the little habitation.

'If there's any petrol in it,' he whispered, 'it may prove our salvation.'

Cautiously he opened the gate, and

with the others at his heels made his way towards the machine. It was an ancient Ford, rusty and almost paintless — but obviously still in use.

'Get in,' he said, opening the door to the back seat, and Colgate-Jones, Peter and Mary squeezed themselves into the interior. Getting up behind the wheel Dene turned on the petrol tap, pressed down the switch and thrust in the starter.

It whined shrilly, but the engine failed to pick up. He tried again, with success. The engine roared to life. Letting on the clutch he sent the car jerking forward towards the gate.

As he did so a chorus of shouting reached him from the way they had come. He smiled grimly as he pressed his foot down harder on the accelerator. The discovery of the car had only just been in time. A volley of shots hummed and whined wickedly around them; then in a few seconds they were out of range, heading along an unknown road to safety!

27

The Sixth Clue

Michael Dene looked up from behind the desk in his office at Whitehall at Peter and Colgate-Jones.

'Two more sections,' he said, 'and the document which poor Jordan wrote before he died will be complete.'

It was late in the evening following their escape from the Moor House. With the aid of the car which Dene had appropriated, they had succeeded in reaching Thirsk. Here the ancient Ford had been left at a garage and they had caught the first available train to York. After a substantial breakfast at the Station Hotel in the Cathedral City, they had been just in time to board the London train and had reached the Metropolis in the early afternoon.

The Secret Service man had deemed it unsafe for Mary Jordan or Colgate-Jones to go back to the vicarage, and had installed them, with Peter Clayton, at a hotel in Charing Cross, concluding rightly that such an establishment was safer than any other. They had arrived in London exhausted and tired, and Mary had gone to bed, after promising Dene that she would not leave the hotel under any pretext whatever, unless she was accompanied by either himself, Colgate-Jones or Peter. He had stipulated for this, and she had agreed readily enough.

When he had arranged with Peter and the clergyman to meet him for dinner he had left to follow up the clue, which he had solved while he lay in the cellar of the house on the Yorkshire Moors.

It had not been difficult to find the 'Golden Gate'. That establishment was a small restaurant among the many which are situated in the neighbourhood of Shaftesbury Avenue, and the head waiter parted readily with the antique snuff-box which Jordan had sent him when Dene explained who he was.

Once in possession of this, it had not taken him long to discover the false bottom which concealed one of the familiar strips, and when he had found this he had sought the rest and sleep which his worn-out body and brain craved.

At a quarter to eight he had awakened, bathed and dressed, and kept his appointment with Colgate-Jones and Peter. After dining at the hotel, and learning that Mary was still asleep, he had brought them back to the office in Whitehall, admitting them by an entrance which opened into a side street and which was known only to himself and such officials who worked in his department. He had a pretty shrewd idea that the front entrance would be closely watched by emissaries of the group which he was fighting, for he guessed that, having lost him after his escape from the Manor House, they would make every effort to find him again.

With the two strips which Dene had got from the pawnshop and the head waiter at the 'Golden Gate' added, Jordan's document read as follows:

In case of my death I wish to
the result of my discoveries dur . . .
years. There is a conspiracy ag . . .

which will culminate on July 27th
The people behind this plot are a
They have acquired from a Polish
invention which has the power to
their intention is to use it agai . . .
reserve, thus ruining the country's
it at the mercy of any of the
the event of war.
For fifteen years they have been
gold reserve of their own which
a place somewhere in the Yorks . . .
have not been able to discover
and when the country is ruined
to come forward and save it
The names of the six men who form
Paul Lenoir, Adolph von Beck, Benito
Wu Li Fu and Morgan Stenson. The
the organiser of the plot and the
The final meeting of these six w . . .
July 27th at Stel Water Manor, Sten . . .
Buckinghamshire. I am coming to Eng . . .
evidence before the British Govern . . .
this plot, but in case my death s . . .
being able to have taken this prec . . .

'It still doesn't carry us very far,'
remarked the Secret Service man. 'It is

most important we find the two final ones.' He picked up his pipe and began to fill it from the jar before him. 'In the meantime let's turn our attention to Jordan's penultimate puzzle; here it is. See what you can make of it.' He picked up the fifth strip and passed it to Colgate-Jones.

The clergyman read the rhyme on the back, with Peter peering over his shoulder:

'The name is legion, the number seven.
Add enough to make eleven.
This will give the street, and then
The number follows, south-west ten.'

'A nice little pill!' growled Peter. 'How the dickens Jordan ever thought of all these things beats me!'

'That's the easiest of the lot,' said Dene quietly, as he applied a match to the bowl of his pipe.

Colgate-Jones looked up.

'You mean you've solved it?' he inquired.

The Secret Service man nodded.

'Yes,' he replied. 'It's really very simple. In fact, it's so simple that it makes me wonder whether Jordan wasn't getting a little careless towards the end.'

'Maybe it's simple to you,' said Peter, shaking his head, 'but I'm hanged if it is to me. What does it mean?'

'It means exactly what it says,' said Michael Dene. 'Possibly that's why you find it difficult. You're looking for a hidden meaning all the time — there isn't one.'

Colgate-Jones wrinkled his brows.

'I don't quite understand you,' he said.

'Well,' the Secret Service man got up and came round behind them, 'the name is legion, the number seven. Add enough to make eleven.' Seven is the number of the house, if you add enough to make eleven you get four, which is the name of a street in West Kensington, the south-west ten district. It's spelt F,O,R,E. Fore Street. The inhabitants of number seven Fore Street, West Kensington, S.W.10, are, according to the London Directory, named Legion. Simple, isn't it?'

The Clergyman grunted.

'Simple enough when you explain,' he said. 'All the same, I think it's pretty smart of you to work it out so quickly. You haven't been to this place?'

Dene shook his head.

'No. I'm going first thing in the morning,' he said.

'Well, after that,' remarked Peter, 'there's only one more to find and then our job's done!'

'You mean it's just started,' corrected Michael Dene. 'I assure you, Clayton, that the most difficult part of this business is yet to come. Even when we know what this conspiracy is and the names of the people responsible for it, we've got to find proof before we can move.'

'Jordan's document — ' began Peter, but Dene interrupted him.

'One man's written statement without evidence to back it up,' he said. 'It's not sufficient. It would carry no weight in a court of law. These men whom he mentions here,' — he tapped the strips on the blotting pad — 'are powerful. Paul Lenoir is one of the richest men in France; Adolph von Beck is the Rockefeller of Germany; Wu Li Fu and Morgan Stenson between them have control of millions, and there are two more whose names we do not know yet but who, without a doubt, are equally important. If we moved against them without proof we should raise an outcry that might precipitate the whole of Europe into war. We've got to move warily. We cannot afford to take one step without absolute and irrefutable proof!'

Colgate-Jones saw the force of his argument and pursed his lips.

'How do you propose to get that?' he asked.

'The proof we need,' said Dene, 'should be available when this meeting takes place at Stenson's house on July the twenty-seventh.'

'But,' protested Peter, 'that bald-headed brute must have read Jordan's statement! He'll know that we are in possession of the fact that this meeting is to take place. Surely they'd alter their plans!'

'They may alter the place, but I doubt if they'll alter the date,' said the Secret Service man. 'I'm of the opinion that their arrangements have gone too far. Anyway, Morgan Stenson is being very closely watched by one of the most competent men in the

Service. The others who constitute the group are not as yet in England. They will be coming over for this meeting, and as each arrives he will be picked up and followed. If there's any alteration in the arrangements I shall know of it.' The telephone bell rang and he picked up the receiver. 'Hello!' he called. 'Yes, Dene speaking.'

For some time he listened, his face expressionless, jotting down notes on a pad at his elbow, and when he put the receiver back on its rack his lips were compressed.

'That was from Scotland Yard,' he said. 'The Yorkshire police, on my information, raided the Moor House an hour ago. The place was deserted, and there was not a speck of gold to be found.'

Peter raised his eyebrows.

'They must have worked quickly to have got all that away in the time,' he remarked.

'You can bet your life they did work quickly!' said Dene. 'The order went out to vacate the Moor House and move its contents immediately it was discovered we'd got away.'

'I wonder what that store of gold was for?' said Colgate-Jones thoughtfully.

'It's evidently part of the great scheme,' said Michael Dene. 'Jordan mentions it here. 'They have been . . . gold reserves of their own . . . ' Guessing at the missing portions, it appears to me that the conspiracy centres round a plot to ruin the country and then come forward and save it. How they propose to achieve that object we can't tell until we get hold of the rest of Jordan's document. That is our most pressing problem at the moment. There is another of equal importance.'

'What's that?' demanded Peter.

'To keep alive until the twenty-seventh!' said Michael Dene grimly.

28

The Explosion

The heat wave, which was destined to culminate in a storm that the newspapers unanimously declared was the worst the country had experienced for over a hundred years, began on the following morning. During the night the temperature rose rapidly and by noon had reached ninety degrees in the shade.

London lay baking under the intense heat; perspiring men stripped their coats in the city, and others more fortunate sought relief in the swimming pools and public parks. Those who were able to hurried to the coast. Theatres and picture houses were empty, and the ice-cream vendors and soda fountains did a roaring trade.

Peter Clayton, Colgate-Jones and Mary Jordan remained at the hotel under the guard, although they did not know it, of unobtrusive men who hung about the vestibule and loitered in the streets nearby, keeping a watchful eye on all and sundry.

Peter had resumed his normal personality, for Dene had considered the disguise of Harry Pinner no longer necessary. That piece of strategy was only useful before their adversaries became aware that the real reason for Jordan's death was known. In the circumstances Peter was delighted, for he was sufficiently immodest to consider himself not ill-looking, and the personality of Harry Pinner, so far as outward appearances went, was anything but prepossessing. Since an increasing interest in the girl rendered it essential that he should look his best, he had hailed his restoration with joy, a joy that had been in no way diminished by Mary Jordan's expression when she had seen him for the first time as he really was.

It's true that there still lingered in his hair traces of the fiery red which had been one of the outstanding features of Mr. Pinner, but otherwise he was normal.

Perhaps of all of them he was most reconciled to the period of inaction that followed, for he was content to spend long hours talking to the girl or taking her for occasional walks in the park. These outings were strictly limited, for Dene was fully aware that Morgan Stenson and his satellites would be straining every nerve to find them and he wished to run no risks. That he was right was proved later.

On the morning following his talk with Peter and Colgate-Jones in the Whitehall office, he had located the Legions of Fore Street, West Kensington, and discovered them to be the proprietors of a respectable boarding house where, apparently, Jordan had stayed several times.

The sixth strip had been concealed in the stem of a large and beautifully carved pipe, which the dead man had sent to Mr. Legion, accompanied by the usual letter, asking him to take care of it until such time as he should either come himself or send someone to collect it.

Michael Dene, in the privacy of Colgate-Jones' bedroom that night, fitted the six strips together, and with a grave face showed the result to his two companions.

'At last,' he said, 'even without the final section, we have sufficient to reveal the diabolical scheme which these people have hatched.'

It was the first inkling that the clergyman and Peter had received of the plot, which a group of power-crazed financiers had conceived against the welfare of Great Britain and the Empire, and they were aghast at the magnitude of the idea.

Without the final section Jordan's strip read:

In case of my death I wish to leave o . . .
the result of my discoveries during the
years. There is a conspiracy against Gr . . .
which will culminate on July 27th of
    this
The people behind this plot are a group
men whose object is power and an immens . . .
They have acquired from a Polish scien-
    tis . . .
invention which has the power to destroy
    g . . .

their intention is to use it against Engl . . .
reserve, thus ruining the country's credit
a . . .
it at the mercy of any of the other p . . .
the event of war.
For fifteen years they have been amassing
gold reserve of their own which is secr . . .
a place somewhere in the Yorkshire Moo . . .
have not been able to discover the exa . . .
and when the country is ruined they will
to come forward and save it at a pr . . .
The names of the six men who form this
g . . .
Paul Lenoir, Adolph von Beck, Benito
Carillo, Elm . . .
Wu Li Fu and Morgan Stenson. The
last n . . .
organiser of the plot and the controlling
The final meeting of these six will take
July 27th, at Stel Water Manor, Stenson's
country
Buckinghamshire. I am coming to England
to la . . .
evidence before the British Government
and
this plot, but in case my death should

        pre . . .
being able to I have taken this precaution.

                    NORRIS JOR . . .

'It doesn't leave much to the imagination, does it?' commented Dene. 'It's
fairly easy to fill in the blanks that are
missing.'

'It's incredible!' breathed Colgate-
Jones, and his face was grave and worried.
'If they are in a position to carry out this
infernal plot, the country would never
recover from the disaster! Think what it
means! The whole of the Empire's credit
would crumble to nothing! Treasury notes
and banknotes would not be worth the
paper they were printed on, they would
be of less value than the German mark
was following the war. The entire country
would be ruined. The present programme
of rearmament would come to a stop
— everything would come to a stop. It
would be the end of the British Empire!'

'And when that has been accom-
plished,' said the Secret Service man
gravely, 'these people will come forward

and offer to replace the gold they have destroyed with their own secret store. They would be in a position to demand practically anything. And not only that, they would hold the country at their mercy, at the mercy of any power with whom they liked to form an alliance!'

'That accounts for those boxes in the cellar of the Moor House,' said Peter, and Dene nodded.

'It must be stopped, Dene!' said Colgate-Jones pacing up and down his room with short, irregular strides. 'It must be stopped at all costs! Can't these six men be arrested?'

'On what charge?' asked the Secret Service man.

'On a charge of conspiracy,' said Colgate-Jones. 'With plotting against the welfare of the country!'

'We've no proof that they are,' said Michael Dene. 'Jordan knew and we know, because I'm prepared to believe that every word that Jordan wrote is true, but we couldn't make anyone else believe it.'

'What do you intend to do then?' asked the clergyman.

'Wait!' said Dene. 'It's the only thing

we can do. Wait until the twenty-seventh of July, when this business comes to a head.'

'I suppose,' remarked Peter, 'there's no doubt that this invention really works? That it does possess the power of destroying gold? It seems incredible to me!'

'All inventions seem incredible,' said Dene, 'until familiarity makes them commonplace. Wireless was incredible at the beginning, so was flying. I don't think we can rely upon there being anything wrong with the invention — whatever it is. You can be certain that it has been thoroughly tested because it forms the basis of the whole scheme. Without it there would be no scheme.'

His eyes were tired, and there were lines of weariness on his face.

'Our only chance,' he went on, 'is to catch these people red-handed, to secure irrefutable proof that will admit of no denial! Tomorrow I have an appointment with the Foreign Secretary, and if I can make him see eye to eye with me and consent to my suggestion. I think we shall achieve our object and prevent this conspiracy from reaching fruition.'

'What's the idea?' asked Peter, but Dene shook his head.

'I'd rather not discuss it with you at the moment,' he said. 'Until I have consulted Lord Weldon, I think it will be better to keep it to myself.'

'I hope,' grunted Colgate-Jones feelingly, 'that you're not going to leave us out? I feel that I owe these people a bit personally.'

Michael Dene smiled.

'I won't leave you out,' he promised. 'You shall have your chance of being in at the death.'

Into the Secret Service man's mind came a mental picture of the misery and ruin that would result should the plot which Jordan's tireless efforts had unearthed became successful. Stocks and shares would crumble; big men and small men, directors of large companies, owners of small businesses, all would be caught up in the general ruin. Clerks and labourers, typists and dock-hands, every condition of worker would be unemployed. Riots and suicides would sweep the country . . .

Michael Dene's teeth clenched and his mouth set. It must never happen! No matter how or in what way — it must be prevented! Civilisation as they knew it was at stake.

He had been standing silently by the window, and now he turned.

'Jordan's last section has yet to be found,' he said. 'If you want something to exercise your minds, try to puzzle out the meaning of his last clue.'

Peter picked up the sixth strip and turned it over. Aloud he read the rhyme on the back:

'The seventh, and please note the last,
Is with a man whose three score years
   are past.
A snob he is, and yet of lowly stock,
Sheer luck will find him if you know
which word to dock.'

'I suppose you've solved this?' said Peter, as be looked up.

Dene shook his head.

'No, I haven't,' he replied. 'To be quite

candid, it's rather beaten me.'

With knit brows Peter and the clergy-man bent over the scrawled lines of writing. Five minutes passed and then Peter shook his head.

'I'm afraid it's beaten me, too,' he confessed.

'And me,' said Colgate-Jones. 'But then I never was much good at this kind of thing.'

Dene said nothing. He was standing, an intent expression on his face, listening.

'What is it?' inquired Peter.

'I was wondering,' said the Secret Service man, 'where the clock is.'

Colgate-Jones stared at him as if he had taken leave of his senses.

'Clock?' he echoed. 'What clock?'

'Can't you hear it?' said Dene, and now that he drew their attention to the sound they were able to make out the soft, rhythmic ticking that came from some-where in the room.

'I don't know what it can be,' said the clergyman. 'There's no clock here, it's the one thing I can't stand in a bedroom, it keeps me awake — '

'You're sure there's no clock?' broke in Dene sharply. 'You haven't a travelling clock in your bag?'

'I haven't even a bag,' Colgate-Jones reminded him humorously, and Dene remembered that, of course, he had brought no luggage.

He had located the sound now; it came from the big wardrobe facing the door.

Quickly he went over, and after listening for a second jerked open the long drawer that occupied the bottom of the piece of furniture. Even as he did so the ticking changed. There was a click, followed by a faint whirring sound.

Dene straightened up, his face white.

'Run!' he shouted. 'Get out for your lives! It's a bomb!'

The others sprang to their feet and made a dash for the door, with Dene at their heels.

They had barely reached the passage outside when a deafening explosion shook the building. A cloud of acrid smoke billowed out from the room they had just left, and the door, blown off its hinges, crashed into the opposite wall of the corridor. There was a rumbling sound of falling brickwork, followed by the crackling of burning wood.

The force of the explosion had flung them to the ground, and as they rose shakily they looked at each other.

'Another minute,' muttered Dene, 'and our friends would have won.'

It was not until some time later that he thought of turning the attempt on their lives to his own advantage.

29

Interlude

EXPLOSION AT WEST END HOTEL! THREE MEN KILLED!

Michael Dene saw the screaming head-lines on the front page of his morning paper, read the account below and smiled with satisfaction. The press had risen nobly to the occasion. While the fire brigade was coping with the flames caused by the bursting of the bomb, the Secret Service man had slipped away to the telephone, and the long conversation he had held with a high official at Scotland Yard had resulted in an urgent request by the police to every newspaper editor in London.

How the group had succeeded in tracing them to the hotel Dene was unable to guess, but the means by which the bomb had been planted in Colgate-Jones' wardrobe was less difficult. One of the waiters, an

Italian, was missing. He had been engaged temporarily to take the place of another man who had stayed away through illness, and there was little doubt that it had been he who had been responsible for the infernal machine.

The false reports of their deaths, Dene concluded, would lull their adversaries into a feeling of false security and make easier the plan that he had in mind. Guessing that the hotel would be under observation, he had smuggled Colgate-Jones, Peter, Mary and himself out by the back entrance, leaving inside a trade delivery van and being set down at Waterloo Station.

His immediate problem had been to find somewhere that could be used as temporary headquarters. The Whitehall office was barred, as was his flat. It was essential that the people he was up against should believe him dead, and he couldn't afford to take any risks that might upset his plan.

It was late when an idea suggested itself to him, and he telephoned the private residence of an estate agent friend of his.

This gentleman lived at Highgate and, hiring a car from a nearby garage, Dene drove out with his companions to see him. Two hours later he was the temporary tenant of a furnished bungalow on the outskirts of Epping Forest.

'I'm afraid,' he said, when they had inspected their new home, 'that we shall have to shift for ourselves. We can't run the risks of engaging servants.'

'I can do all the cooking that's necessary,' volunteered Mary, and the new household came into being.

Early on the following morning Peter went into Epping and ordered a stock of supplies, bringing back sufficient with him for breakfast. The weather was still hot and, according to the reports, likely to continue so.

Dene spent the greater part of the day puzzling over Jordan's last rhyme, and by teatime he had succeeded in ferreting out the secret. He went out into the little garden to acquaint the others with his success.

'The person who is holding the last section is a shoemaker who is carrying on business at Shere,' he said.

'How do you make that out?' asked Colgate-Jones.

The Secret Service man explained.

'A 'snob' is another name for a shoemaker,' he said, 'and further confirmation is supplied by the word 'last' at the end of the first line. If you take away 'luck' from 'sheer luck' it leaves Shere — a small village in Surrey. I think I'm right, but I propose going over to Shere immediately after tea and making certain.'

He returned shortly after eight, triumphant. He had found the elderly cobbler, who had been well acquainted with Norris Jordan. The last section of the dead man's statement was concealed in the back of a small picture, a rather attractive water-colour, by a Belgian artist, which he had sent to the old man for safe keeping.

Dene pieced the seven strips together and read Jordan's completed statement:

In case of my death I wish to leave on record

the result of my discoveries during the
     past ten
years. There is a conspiracy against Great
     Britain
which will culminate on July 27th of
     this year.
The people behind this plot are a group
     of rich
men whose object is power and an immense
     fortune.
They have acquired from a Polish scien-
     tist an
invention which has the power to destroy
     gold, and
their intention is to use it against England's
     gold
reserve, thus ruining the country's credit
     and placing
it at the mercy of any of the other
     powers in
the event of war.
For fifteen years they have been amass-
     ing a huge
gold reserve of their own which is secreted
     at
a place somewhere in the Yorkshire Moors
     — I

have not been able to discover the exact locality —

and when the country is ruined they will offer

to come forward and save it at a price.

The names of the six men who form this group are

Paul Lenoir, Adolph von Beck, Benito Carillo, Elmer P. Chase,

Wu Li Fu and Morgan Stenson. The last named is

the organiser of the plot and the controlling brain.

The final meeting of these six will take place on

July 27th at Stel Water Manor, Stenson's country house in

Buckinghamshire. I am coming to England to lay

evidence before the British Government and prevent

this plot, but in case my death should prevent my

being able to I have taken this precaution.

NORRIS JORDAN.

'Benito Carillo and Elmer Chase!' said Michael Dene. 'It's a cosmopolitan crowd, isn't it?'

'Whatever their nationalities,' grunted Colgate-Jones, 'they all serve one master — the devil! Their spiritual country is Hell, and I'd like to see 'em sent there!'

'Maybe you will,' said Dene. 'In the meantime we can do nothing now but wait for the twenty-seventh.'

The days that followed were uneventful. They read and smoked and chatted, seldom going beyond the confines of the bungalow's garden, although Dene was in constant touch with Whitehall and Scotland Yard by telephone.

On the fifth of July a man named Wu Li Fu arrived in London and settled in a palatial suite at the Ritz. On the tenth came Adolph von Beck, his advent heralded by many flourishings of trumpets in the newspapers. On the nineteenth Elmer P. Chase came down the gangway of the White Star liner 'Gigantic' at Southampton, and on the twenty-second Paul Lenoir reached Croydon from Paris and Benito Carillo came from Rome. And each man, as he set foot on English soil, was picked up by two watchers, and from that moment kept under close observation.

Michael Dene's interview with the Foreign Secretary had proved successful, but only after a great deal of difficulty. At first Lord Weldon would not hear of the suggestion which the Secret Service man put up to him, and it was only when the full gravity of the situation had been brought home to him that he reluctantly gave his consent.

On the morning of the twenty-sixth Dene called his friends into conference and gave them their final instructions and in the afternoon of that day left the bungalow at Epping and took train for London.

The heat wave reached its height that night. In London the thermometer stood at ninety-four degrees, and there was no air to relieve the temperature.

'It can't go on,' said the lugubrious Inspector Dilly, when Dene interviewed him in his bare office at Scotland Yard. 'It's bound to break, and when it does there'll be fireworks. You mark my words!'

He spoke prophetically. The end of that period of tropical heat was near at hand, and Dene wondered many times after whether it was a coincidence that it came on the night of July the twenty-seventh.

30

The Night of July the Twenty-seventh

Throughout the morning and afternoon of that twenty-seventh day of July the sun beat down on Stel Water Manor from a sky that was like an inverted bowl of molten copper. Beneath the intense heat the flowers wilted in the borders, and the flagstones of the ruined monastery were so hot at noon that a steak could have been fried with ease upon them. No breath of wind stirred the drooping leaves of the trees in the park, and over everything hung a shimmering haze.

The first signs of the approaching storm came towards six o'clock, when heavy clouds began to bank themselves upon the horizon, thick, woolly clouds, with livid edges, the portent of which there was no mistaking.

From the windows of his big study Morgan Stenson saw them and turned to Voles.

'We're in for a storm,' he said in his high, thin voice. 'And a good thing, too; probably it will break this infernal heat.'

The stout man, tightly collared and suited as usual, in spite of the weather, mopped his face delicately with a silk handkerchief and passed it over the gleaming dome of his naked skull.

'It will be a relief, sir,' he said. 'Maybe it's a good omen.'

'You have prepared the meeting place?' said Stenson, and his secretary nodded.

'Yes, everything is ready,' he replied.

'The others will be here at a quarter to eight,' said his employer. 'We shall dine first and then adjourn to settle the final details of the plan.'

His eyes glittered, and into his pale cheeks crept a little spot of colour.

'The goal is in sight, Voles,' he went on. 'The thing for which I have worked untiringly for fifteen years is about to be made possible. The child of my brain will be born tonight!' He came over to his desk and sat down. 'Three days from now,' he said hoarsely, 'I shall have the country in the hollow of my hands. I shall have achieved power, such as many men have dreamed of but never realised!'

'And you will deserve it, sir,' said the sycophantic Voles. 'No one but you could have conceived such a marvellous idea.'

'No one but I could have carried it out,' said Stenson. 'The lists are all prepared?'

'Yes,' said the bald-headed man. 'Nothing has been forgotten.'

'Good!' Morgan Stenson helped himself to a cigar and lit it slowly with care.

'There is only one thing,' ventured Voles. 'Don't you think it is a risk to hold this meeting here?'

Stenson shook his head.

'Where is the risk?' he demanded. 'The man Dene and his companions are dead, and even if they were still alive what proof have they against us? It doesn't matter if the whole world knows of the meeting here tonight, they will merely imagine that it is a business consultation between business men. It might cause a great deal of talk and speculation in the City if it were known, that is all. Unless someone was actually present at the conference, and that is an impossibility, there is no proof that we are not ordinary financiers discussing ordinary financial business. Apart from that, we have taken the precaution to arrange that the meeting be held in the underground cellar of the ruins. Few people beyond you and I know of its existence. No, we are safe enough! And after the scheme has been put into practice it matters not who knows!'

He snapped his fingers.

'They dare not do anything to any of us then because we shall be omnipotent. We shall be the only people able to dictate terms! Leave me; I want to go over everything in my mind in case any detail has been forgotten. I'll ring if I want you.'

The stout man bowed and withdrew, and until the silvery chimes of a gong warned him that it was time to dress, Morgan Stenson sat motionless, the smoke curling from between his thin lips, his eyes half closed, conning over the details of the scheme which was to bring ruin to his country.

* * *

The five men who came down to the dinner their host provided for them, immaculately clad in evening dress, were so markedly different in outward appearance that the picture they made seated round the polished table lit by the soft light of candles in silver sconces would have gladdened the heart of an artist.

Morgan Stenson himself small and wizened, his sallow skin made sallower by the gleaming white of his collar and shirt front; Rudolph von Beck, fat, perspiring, his neck bulging over the circle of starched linen that surrounded it; Paul Lenoir, slim, sleek and leaden-faced, with black hair and moustache; the swarthy Benito Carillo, square-jawed, blue-chinned, black-eyed, with curling hair that surrounded a bald spot like the tonsure of a monk; Elmer Chase, lean and dry-looking, with wrinkled chin and rheumy eyes and hands that resembled the talons of a bird of prey; and Wu Li Fu, high cheek-boned and almond-eyed, with the wide nostrils and yellow skin of his race.

No word concerning the real reason for their presence was uttered during the meal, but the conversation did not languish. Many and varied were the subjects discussed, ranging from art to literature, sport and politics. Had anyone been present they would merely have concluded that it was an ordinary social gathering of rich and powerful men who had met to enjoy themselves and perhaps, incidentally, conclude some important business deal.

It was not until after coffee and liqueurs had been served and the servants had withdrawn that anything was said to contradict this supposition, and then glancing at his watch, Morgan Stenson looked at the faces before him.

'Gentlemen,' he said, 'when you have finished your coffee we will adjourn to a more private place and begin the real business for which we have met.'

There was an appreciative murmur, and as it died away the first rumble of distant thunder, the herald of the storm that was to sweep the country and rage without cessation for twelve hours, came to their ears. Morgan Stenson glanced through the windows. Outside, dusk had begun to mingle with the curious blue-tinted light of the earlier evening, a dusk rendered strange and peculiar by reason of the coppery hue that invaded it.

Again the muttering rumble sounded.

'I guess it will be a good thing,' said the American. 'Clear the air. It's like a Turkish bath tonight.'

'It will be cool enough where we are going,' said Stenson

'What is this place of which you speak?' asked Lenoir. 'Why cannot we hold our discussion in your study?'

'Because the place I have prepared is more private,' answered his host, 'and, as I said, cooler.'

'We have a journey to go?' inquired the Chinaman, and his English was that of the University at which he had received his education.

'Not far,' said Stenson, and again the low rumbling like distant guns, dovetailed into his words.

They finished their coffee and liqueurs and lit the cigars, which a servant brought in. There was a curious sense of tension in the atmosphere that was not entirely attributable to the coming storm, a tension and, with all of them, an air of expectancy.

It was half-past nine when Morgan Stenson rose to his feet.

'Let me show you round the garden, gentlemen,' he said, and pushed open the big French windows that opened on to the terrace.

There was a hush in the air, an absolute and complete stillness that pervaded everything, as though all motion in the world had ceased and it was holding its breath. The pallid, ochre-hued light held something sinister as he led the way down the steps and across the smooth-shaven lawn. Passing through the rose garden he opened a gate.

'The going is rather difficult here,' he apologised, and there was reason, for rank grass and undergrowth grew in profusion, through which protruded heaps of grey stone.

Before them rose the truncated tower of the ruined monastery, to one side of which a great arch, ivy-covered and blotched with lichen, marked the entrance through which the ancient monks had returned from their labours. They passed through and found themselves on flagstones, moss covered, through the cracks of which weeds grew. Voles was waiting in the dimness and led them over to a corner where a huge stone trap stood open.

'The vaults,' said Morgan Stenson, 'were the only things left when the building was destroyed. They are practically as intact now as they were at the time they were built.'

The bald-headed man switched on a powerful electric torch and as they began to descend, the first of those sudden fierce gusts of seemingly directionless wind came flying through the trees of the wood, on the fringe of which the ruins lay, and with it the pattering smack of large isolated raindrops.

At the bottom of the stone steps was an archway leading into a big vaulted chamber, in the centre of which had been placed a table and six chairs. It was lighted by two petrol vapour lamps that stood at each end of the table, and Morgan Stenson ushered his guests into the chairs that had been placed for them.

'We are completely safe here from interruption,' he said, as he took his own place at the end of the table. 'The stone flag by which we entered is the only means of egress, and since my secretary, Voles, who as you know is entirely in our confidence, will be on watch throughout this conference, there can be no danger of any unauthorised eavesdropper. Let us get to business.

'It is unnecessary for me to go into the reason for this meeting; that you already know. All I have to inform you is that the details are complete, and we are ready to put the plan into immediate execution.'

'The invention has proved a success?' asked the Chinaman softly.

'A complete success!' said Stenson. 'Dostoviski has improved on the original plan which I succeeded in obtaining from that dying Pole in Budapest. The ray will destroy gold, reduce it to a heap of crumbling white powder, no matter in what receptacle it may be contained. It penetrates concrete, glass and steel, and has no effect on any other metal except gold.'

'What is the range of the instrument?'

asked the American.

'The range depends on the size and power,' replied Stenson, 'but for our purpose I considered half a mile sufficient, and so the instruments have been made to cover that range. They can be carried in an ordinary motor car, and our agents in the Colonies are already in receipt of the necessary number for our purpose. I have here,' — he opened a folder in front of him — 'a list of every gold depository in the British Empire. On the date agreed upon our agents will be notified and every particle of gold will be destroyed! The apparatus will be carried in closed cars. In less than six hours from the receipt of our instructions by our agents every particle of gold in the British Empire — with the exception of our own reserve, which I had to remove from the house in Yorkshire and bring here — will be destroyed! It will be impossible to hush up the disaster. The country will be ruined; the markets will crumble; the pound will be valueless!'

'And then we step in!' grunted the American.

'Germany steps in,' growled von Beck, his small eyes gleaming. 'We dictate terms to these British!'

'And they are bound to accept whatever we demand,' said Stenson, 'for we shall be all-powerful! We shall be the rulers of Great Britain! And not only that. If we like, if we extend our operations, we can become the rulers of the world, for we have it in our power to destroy the commerce of the world — '

His words were drowned in a shattering roar that ended in a long, rolling echo.

'We shall hold,' cried Stenson, his voice rising to a thin scream, 'the life or death of civilisation in the hollow of our hands, and nobody can touch us! Nobody dare touch us! Once we have put this scheme into execution, and it remains now but for us to agree upon a date, we shall be immune from the law, immune from everything! Invulnerable! Untouchable!'

'But the plan will never be put into execution.' said Wu Li Fu calmly, and there was an automatic pistol in each of his hands. 'You are under arrest, the lot of you, for conspiring against the welfare of Great Britain! Put up your hands!'

They swung round as he rose and backed towards the arched entrance. The face was still the face of the Chinaman, but the voice was that of Michael Dene, of the Secret Service!

31

The Vengeance of the Storm

'Dene!' hissed Morgan Stenson, when he recovered from his first shock. 'Dene! I thought you were dead! Where's Wu Li Fu?'

'At the present moment sleeping peacefully at the Ritz under the guard of two men from Scotland Yard!' snapped Michael Dene. 'His coffee at lunch was doped and injections will be administered at intervals to keep him unconscious. I was afraid you might miss him and so I took his place. He will wake up in less comfortable surroundings than the bedroom he now occupies.'

They glared at him speechless.

'What is this, a trap?' snarled von Beck. 'Who is this man, Stenson?'

It was Dene who answered.

'I have the honour,' he said, 'to be at the head of the Special Branch of the

Secret Service. It may interest you gentlemen to know that ever since you landed in England you have been trailed and for days past this house has been kept under observation. Your secretary, Voles, was seen preparing this place, and precautions were taken to ensure that sufficient evidence would be collected to offer irrefutable proof of your connection with this business. A microphone has been installed in this vault, and every word that has been uttered has been recorded. When you come up for trial, Stenson, your own words in your own voice will convict you.'

'I shall never come up for trial!' screamed the millionaire, and with a supreme effort he overturned the table.

It went over with a crash, smashing the two petrol lamps and extinguishing them. Dene expected the concerted rush that followed and sprang nimbly for the stone steps. Leaping up them he swung the heavy stone down and sent it thudding into place, bottling up the five men effectually. He gave a soft whistle, and Peter, Colgate-Jones and the lugubrious Dilly appeared from the shadow of the woods.

'You've got Voles?' snapped Dene, and the Scotland Yard man nodded.

'Yes, we got him,' he said. 'The others down there?'

'They're all right,' said Dene. 'Was the man who was recording Stenson's little piece successful?'

'We got every word,' said Peter, and Dene gave an exclamation of satisfaction.

'Fetch your men, Dilly,' he began, 'and we'll get them out. There's — '

What he was going to say he never said. The sky was rent with a vivid flash of blue-white flame and a peal of thunder that shook the earth beneath their feet went crashing and echoing over their heads. In a deluge the rain came down, hissing and splashing around them and soaking them to the skin in less than two seconds.

A second flash and a second crash of thunder and then a yellow white ball of fire leaped from the sky and struck downwards towards the truncated tower of the ruined monastery. A blinding glare of blue-white light seared their eyes and for a second they were surrounded by crackling fire.

With a cry Michael Dene leaped back, and as he did so he saw what was left of the tower totter and fall, crashing across the stone trap near which, a moment earlier, he had been standing.

'My God, what was that?' gasped Peter.

'A thunderbolt!' said the Secret Service man shakily. 'A thunderbolt that has destroyed all necessity for any evidence against the five men who are buried down there!'

★ ★ ★

The green of summer had faded to the gold of autumn and there was a tang in the air, when Peter Clayton and the girl on whom he had just bestowed his name came out of the little church at Claybury and stepped into the waiting car that was to take them to the station.

'Well, goodbye and good luck!' said Colgate-Jones, his jovial face wreathed in smiles. 'Don't forget I shall expect you to keep your word and spend Christmas at the vicarage. Dene's promised to come down, haven't you, Dene?'

The Secret Service man nodded.

'Unless anything happens to prevent it,' he said. 'You must realise that my time is not entirely my own. I am more or less at the disposal of the department.'

'We'll come anyway,' said Peter, 'won't we, Mary?'

The girl nodded, smiling.

The car began to move, and Dene and the clergyman watched it, waving a last farewell as it disappeared round a bend in the road.

'Come back to the vicarage,' he said, 'and have a drink.'

Michael Dene agreed.

'You know,' Colgate-Jones continued, as they strolled along together, 'I'm glad Mary's married; she needed someone to look after her, and Clayton's a decent chap.' He sighed as they turned in at the vicarage gate.

'Why the sigh?' asked Dene.

Colgate-Jones shrugged his shoulders.

'I don't know — ' he began, and then: 'Yes, I do, though. I was thinking. You know it's going to seem a little dull after the excitement I've been through.'

Dene laughed. 'Personally I could do with a little dullness for a change!' he remarked.

There was a hint of enviousness in the look the clergyman gave him.

'Excitement's part of your existence,' he said, 'but with me — well, well, mustn't grumble, and by Jove, that was the finest holiday I ever had!'

THE END

We do hope that you have enjoyed reading this large print book.

Did you know that all of our titles are available for purchase?

We publish a wide range of high quality large print books including:
Romances, Mysteries, Classics
General Fiction
Non Fiction and Westerns

Special interest titles available in large print are:
The Little Oxford Dictionary
Music Book, Song Book
Hymn Book, Service Book

Also available from us courtesy of Oxford University Press:
Young Readers' Dictionary
(large print edition)
Young Readers' Thesaurus
(large print edition)

For further information or a free brochure, please contact us at:
Ulverscroft Large Print Books Ltd.,
The Green, Bradgate Road, Anstey,
Leicester, LE7 7FU, England.
Tel: (00 44) 0116 236 4325
Fax: (00 44) 0116 234 0205

Other titles in the
Linford Mystery Library:

DEATH IN THE SQUARE

Ardath Mayhar

The upper-class inhabitants of the locked-
gate commu   quare
in Templeto   their
sedate, priva   ually
private dark   them
keeps hidden   when
a vicious blac   upts
their existenc   mur-
dered in the   nust
be called. N   :hief
Wash Shipp c   and
save their tatte